Dan cleared his throat. "Are you sure this is a good idea?" he asked.

The pen dropped onto the wooden bar as Sophie pulled away from him. "What else am I meant to do?" she asked, her gaze focused everywhere but at him. "I don't want to go to the wedding alone and the only single man I know in Perth is *you*. And you won't do it."

"I'll do it," he said.

Finally she met his gaze, her eyes wide. "You and I," she said, pointing at Dan, then at herself, then back at him, "would never, ever work."

Even though he agreed, her rebuff was a shock to his system. Women rarely…actually, *never* rejected him.

"I'd agree," he said, "if this were genuine. But it's not. And we're adults. We can separate the fake from the real."

Very slowly, she nodded. "Okay. I should be able to get the money transferred early next week—"

"I don't want your money," he said.

Now she looked as shocked as he assumed he had a few minutes earlier.

"Then why would you do it?"

He had no idea. It was a mistake, and he knew it. The chemistry between them was too palpable, and the last thing Sophie needed was a guy like him. A guy whose longest relationship in the past ten years had lasted just over a month.

He was not the one to give Sophie her faith back in men.

But of course—that wasn't what he'd just offered to do.

Dear Reader,

I started writing this book while visiting Vela Luka, a picturesque town on the island of Korcula, Croatia. I'd become engaged just weeks earlier, and was still at the stage where I'd stare at the ring on my finger and smile. Actually, I still do that!

I couldn't have asked for more romantic inspiration, could I? But back then all I had was the opening line (I'll let you turn the page to see what that is!). Who was the woman who'd said that? And why? Well, once I knew why Sophie said what she did, I just had to write her happy-ever-after, even though I knew it was going to be a little bit different.

Secrets and Speed Dating was the winner of the 2010 Harlequin Mills & Boon New Voices U.K. competition. Winning the competition was one of the most unexpected and thrilling experiences of my life.

I'd like to thank everyone who was brave enough to enter New Voices, and every single person who voted for my entry. You've made my dream of publication come true.

And if you're meeting Sophie and Dan for the first time, I hope you enjoy their story. As the stars of my first published novel, they will always be special to me.

Leah

LEAH ASHTON

Secrets and Speed Dating

TORONTO NEW YORK LONDON
AMSTERDAM PARIS SYDNEY HAMBURG
STOCKHOLM ATHENS TOKYO MILAN MADRID
PRAGUE WARSAW BUDAPEST AUCKLAND

Recycling programs
for this product may
not exist in your area.

ISBN-13: 978-0-373-17815-5

SECRETS AND SPEED DATING

First North American Publication 2012

An unashamed fan of all things happily-ever-after, **Leah Ashton** has been a lifelong reader of romance. Writing came a little bit later—although, in hindsight she's been dreaming up stories for as long as she can remember. Sadly, the most popular boy in school never did suddenly fall head over heels in love with her....

Now she lives in Perth, Western Australia, with her own real-life hero, two gorgeous dogs and the world's smartest cat. By day she works in IT-land; by night she considers herself incredibly lucky to be writing the type of books she loves to read, and to have the opportunity to share her own characters' happy-ever-afters with readers.

You can visit Leah at www.leah-ashton.com.

Secrets and Speed Dating is Leah Ashton's fabulous first book for Harlequin Romance!

For Linley—who started it all.

I'd like to thank Nikki for—everything. I couldn't have done it without you.

I'd also like to thank my editor, Meg Lewis, for giving me every chance to get this book right. You had faith in me when I didn't.

To the Monday and Tuesday Night Dinner crowds, thank you for the food and for the laughter. I love you all.

And thank you, Regan, for proving to me that heroes really do exist.

CHAPTER ONE

The Sophie Project (Project Manager: S. Morgan)
Task One: Find a boyfriend

'JUST so you know, I can't have children.'

Sophie Morgan watched her date's expression morph from a twinkly-eyed grin to slack-jawed surprise at her calmly delivered statement. She took a sip of her vanilla martini and met his wide eyes as she continued. 'I *really* can't. It wouldn't matter if I "stopped trying" or "went on a holiday" or "just relaxed".' She shrugged. 'It just won't happen.'

Her date had barely blinked, so she gestured vaguely at her flat stomach. 'Things down there just don't function properly...*reproductively* speaking, of course. I mean, I *can* have sex. That's all normal.'

The poor guy spluttered into his beer. 'Ah, isn't this conversation a bit...premature? We've known each other five minutes.'

He was being literal. A moment later the high-pitched chime of a small silver bell silenced the room.

The hostess of the speed dating evening—a depressingly stunning model-type who Sophie was sure would never need to attend such an event herself—waited until all eyes were on her. Unlike Sophie, her hostess looked completely at ease in the *über*-modern bar, with its black granite floor, chrome and glass furniture and leather couches. Back in Sydney, this type of place had been Sophie's domain. But now, in Perth, with her old life three thousand kilometres away, she felt like an impostor.

'Okay, gentlemen, time to say goodbye and move on to your next date.'

Her date still look dazed, so she tried to explain quickly, hopeful that she didn't sound like a completely unbalanced lunatic. She *did* know blurting out her infertility wasn't exactly normal behaviour. 'Look, everyone here wants a relationship, right?'

He nodded. In fact, this speed dating event was specifically for people seeking long-term relationships.

'So, when most people picture a relationship, they want the whole package deal—wife and kids. With me, that's not possible. I just thought it was only fair you should know.'

He shook his head. 'Not everyone wants that. I don't know if I want kids.'

Sophie smiled, but shrugged. 'I still think it's better to be up-front, get it out in the open. What you want now can change a heck of a lot in the future.'

People changed their minds. She knew that far too well.

Her date smiled at her. Reassuringly, he now looked more bemused than ready to run screaming away from her—that twinkle was even back in his eyes. 'Who knows about the future?' he asked as he stood. 'Why not let a new relationship just flow? Why worry about it now?'

She watched him sit down at the neighbouring table, his attention already on his next date. She envied his naivety. The ability to live a relationship in the moment, to pretend that all you needed was each other. But Sophie wouldn't do that again. She couldn't.

Not that she didn't want the fairytale happy ending. She did. She'd love to grow old with her perfect man—whatever that meant. Definitely someone who didn't want kids. And *really* didn't—although she really had no clue how she could unequivocally determine that. Maybe someone who'd already had his children? Or was older? Not that she really went for much older men.

She took another sip of her cocktail, a humourless smile quirking her lips. Clearly she didn't know what she wanted. She just knew that she wasn't about to waste her time—or risk her heart—on some guy who would dump her once he knew what she couldn't give him. Getting it all out up-front was definitely a good idea. An *excellent* idea, even.

Still, when she'd flipped over her date card she quickly circled 'No' beside her last date's name. As she had for the four dates before him, and probably would for the remaining five.

Wait.

No. She needed to—*had to*—think positive.

She wasn't ready to admit that speed dating was a mistake. After all, it was the first task on her list. If she couldn't do this, what chance did the rest of her project have?

And if she knew that dropping her bombshell was abnormal behaviour, she *certainly* knew that the very existence of her project tipped her over the edge into…well…a little bit nutty. Knew it—but was determined to carry on regardless.

After the amorphous, directionless mess of the past six months she needed a goal—needed a *plan*.

Reaching into the handbag hanging on the back of her chair, she ran her finger along the sharply folded edges of the piece of paper that had led her here this evening.

A single piece of paper. Flimsy—it could so easily be crumpled and thrown away. But she wouldn't be doing that. Instead, it gave her focus. Just as when she'd sat down at her laptop and methodically put the document together. Soothing lists of tasks and deliverable dates—familiar in their structure and yet so different in their type and intent from the project plans she was used to. For this time Sophie Morgan, Project Manager, was *not* implementing a major software upgrade, or rolling out new hardware, or co-ordinating a change management program.

No, this time the project was her life. Her *new* life.

Sophie took a deep breath. Straightened her shoulders.

It didn't matter that she didn't know who or what would make her circle 'Yes'. She just owed herself—and her remaining dates—her full attention, and at least the tiniest smidgen of hope. No premature circling of 'No'.

And definitely—*definitely*—still disclosing her…uh… situation.

So far the reaction to her announcement had been almost comically consistent, except for the beer-spluttering of her last date. That had been new—but then so had her rather graphic description. She grinned at the memory. She probably shouldn't have done that, even if her more than slightly sick sense of humour had always helped her deal with her problems, infertility or otherwise. She figured that was healthier than the total denial of her mid-teens to early twenties: *I never wanted kids, anyway. They're just snotty alien spew-makers. Yuk!*

Her next date settled into his seat. Middling height, with bright red hair, he beamed at her, and she couldn't help her grin becoming a smile.

'Hi,' he said, obviously about to launch into a well-practised line. 'Why on earth would a stunningly beautiful woman like yourself need to go speed dating?'

But she laughed anyway, determined to enjoy the next four and a half minutes.

And then she'd let him know.   •

After his third or fourth surreptitious glance, Dan Halliday decided to just give in and look. Something about the woman who'd stayed long after the other speed daters had left kept drawing his attention. Unsurprisingly, the appeal of polishing wine glasses or counting the night's takings really couldn't compete with the beautiful woman propping up his bar.

She was twisted slightly on her seat, so she could stare out of the window that ran the length of the Subiaco Wine Bar. He had the feeling she wasn't people-watching, though, as the one time he'd asked if she wanted another drink he'd felt as if he was interrupting, that she'd been lost in her own little world. He'd left her alone since then—surreptitious glances excluded.

If she *had* been watching she would have seen the constant stream of cars and the packed café tables of a few hours earlier transition into a rowdier, typical Friday night club crowd. The cafés and restaurants that spilled onto the busy city street were now mostly closed, and only the late-night pubs and clubs remained open. His bar needed to close too, and she was the last customer.

Her hair was long, dark blonde, and swept back off her face in a ponytail—which he liked. He'd never understood women who hid behind curtains of hair. This way he had an unrestricted view of her profile: pale, creamy skin with a touch of colour at her cheeks, a long, slightly pointed nose and a chin that hinted at a stubborn streak.

He couldn't tell her height, seated as she was, but he'd guess she was tall. She wore a deep red silky blouse that skimmed the swell of her breasts, and he could just see her crumpled, obviously forgotten speed dating name-tag stuck beside the V of pale skin her top revealed. But he was too far away to read it.

And then she turned her head and locked her gaze with his. 'Are you closed? Do you want me to go?'

Even from where he stood, a few metres away, he was

caught momentarily by the intense colour of her eyes. They were blue—but unlike his own boring plain blue, hers were darker. Richer. More expressive.

He gave himself a mental shake. *Dan Halliday philosophising over the colour of a woman's eyes? Really?*

Dan cleared his throat. 'Yes to the first question, but no to the second. You're welcome to stay and finish your drink.'

'You sure? I must have been here for...' she glanced at her watch '...almost *three* hours, and I've only had half of my cocktail. You could be waiting a while.'

He put down the glass he'd been not polishing while he'd stared—*leered, maybe, Dan?*—and walked to her end of the bar. 'Really, I don't mind. I'll tell you what—how about I give you a fresh cocktail on the house and you can get back to that serious contemplation you looked to be doing while I finish up?'

She shook her head. 'Thank you, but no. I'm sure you don't want me staring out of the window like a zombie any longer. I'll go.'

'So it's all figured out, then?'

Her brow furrowed. 'What is?'

'Whatever it was you were contemplating—it's all sorted? Done and dusted?'

She laughed, but it was a brittle sound. 'No. Not sorted.' She sighed. 'But, trust me, one more cocktail is not going to sort out the total mess of my life.'

Dan knew he should just let her leave. That right about now all his instinctive confirmed bachelor alarm bells should be ringing. This was a woman who had just attended a speed dating evening and had a self-confessed messy life. That was one alarm bell for 'wants a relationship' and another for 'has baggage'. The noise should be deafening.

Instead, he reached for a fresh martini glass, and didn't

bother analysing why he didn't want her to go. 'Stay. Stare like a zombie all you like.'

A moment passed. Then another. But eventually she smiled, and nodded. 'Thank you.'

His gaze flicked to her name tag.

Sophie.

A deep aversion to her mother's inevitable requirement for a blow-by-blow account of her speed dating 'adventure', as her mum insisted on calling it, was the reason Sophie had lingered at the bar. At least that was the original reason. But hours had passed since she'd sent a 'Don't wait up' text message, fully aware she was only delaying the inquisition, and still she didn't go home.

At some point she'd stopped making up stories about the diners she could see through the bar's window. She'd stopped imagining which couples were on a first date, who was out for dinner for their birthday, or who was a tourist. The stories were a habit she'd fallen into over the past few months—an effective distraction from actually thinking. It was far easier to analyse and deconstruct a stranger's life than her own. Even her ill-fated plan had been all about striding forward. She hadn't been brave enough to look back.

But tonight she'd let her eyes unfocus, her vision blur, and for the first time in what felt like for ever had let the jumble of memories in.

Sydney.

Rick.

Rick's new girlfriend.

Rick's new *pregnant* girlfriend.

Lost in thought—in contemplation, she supposed, like the bartender had said—she hadn't noticed the other customers leaving. And somehow—remarkably, really—she hadn't noticed the fact her bartender was drop dead gorgeous.

She'd felt him watching her, but had expected a 'finish your drink and leave' type of glare when she'd looked up. He'd surprised her. He hadn't been glaring—not even close. There'd been undeniable interest in his hooded gaze.

She lifted the fresh martini to her lips and studied him over the rim of the cocktail glass as he methodically counted money from the till. He stood with his hip resting casually against the stainless steel counter, his long legs clad in darkest grey jeans and the breadth of his shoulders emphasised by his fitted black shirt. The sleeves were rolled up, revealing rich olive skin and arms that looked strong—as if he did a lot more than just pour drinks with them.

With his short cropped black hair and sky-blue eyes he was far more handsome than any of her speed dates that evening. Of course it hadn't been her dates' looks, intelligence, charm or even their reaction to her unsolicited medical announcement that had been the problem.

She twisted in her chair so she faced the window again, her back to the bartender. She watched a gaggle of young women spill, laughing, out of a restaurant across the road. Hmm— Maybe they were on a hen's night? Or maybe they worked together and were having particularly enthusiastic Friday night drinks?

No. Focus. Her free drink was for contemplation, not day-dreaming.

Okay. The problem was that she'd been wrong. She just wasn't ready for a relationship.

Her bruised heart didn't care that she had a perfectly scheduled five-week plan practically burning a hole in her handbag. It turned out that, no matter how hard she tried, she wasn't able to self-impose a 'get over it' or 'move on' deadline.

So, sexy bartender or not, she'd take his offer at face value:

continue her zombie-like staring out of the window, finish her drink, then leave.

'How's that contemplation going?'

Sophie jumped, surprised to hear him so close. She looked over her shoulder to see him wiping down the bar.

'Fine, thanks! Plus I've nearly finished my drink, so I'm almost out of your hair.' She held up her near-empty glass in demonstration, then turned back to her window.

'Anything you want to talk about?'

She spun around in her seat at that, ignoring the concerned look in his eyes. 'Nope!'

She gulped the rest of her martini and plonked the empty glass down a little too hard on the bar's polished surface.

The bartender raised his eyebrows. 'I've owned this bar for ten years. Trust me, I know when someone needs to talk.'

Sophie slid off the barstool, slung her handbag over her shoulder and headed for the exit. The click of her heels echoed in the near-empty room. A cleaner swept near the door, but he paused to open it for her.

She wasn't sure what she'd expected. That he'd follow her? Tell her to stop?

The fact that he did neither, and that of course he wouldn't—she was a total stranger!—made her pause.

She couldn't unload to her mother and sister. They were too quick to interject, to judge. Too desperate to give her a solution when all she wanted was someone to listen.

The temptation to talk to the bartender—a man who didn't know her, whom she was unlikely to see again—was too strong to ignore.

She turned and walked back to the bar.

He was calmly polishing a wine glass.

Sophie took a deep breath. 'My fiancé dumped me two months before my wedding.'

He didn't say anything for a moment. He just looked at her, as if he was thinking something over.

'Ouch,' he finally replied. 'Let me get you another drink.'

CHAPTER TWO

The Sophie Project (Project Manager: S. Morgan)
Task One: Find a boyfriend date?

THE words hadn't come tentatively. Not at all. Instead they'd leapt, tripped and tumbled in a big, rambling rush from her mouth, desperate to be heard.

Sophie wasn't sure how long she'd been talking, but she'd talked *a lot*. More than she had in six months—probably way more than the bartender had expected. Poor guy. He sat beside her on a barstool, still drinking his first bourbon and coke, his jean-clad knee only a few inches from her own. Earlier he'd switched off most of the lights, so the room was lit only by the soft, multicoloured glow of the backlit rows of spirits and liqueurs lining the wall behind the bar.

Now the bartender knew Rick had ditched her for another woman—a work colleague of theirs, no less. He knew she'd had to leave her job, as working with her ex and his new girlfriend each day was—obviously—not an option. He knew she'd sold her share of the house to Rick and promptly spent all her money backpacking through Asia. And he knew that, with barely a cent to her name, and no job or home to return to, here she was back in Western Australia. Living with her well-meaning, wonderful, but suffocating, mother.

But she hadn't told him it all. Of all the things she'd told him, she'd withheld what she'd told every other man that evening. Why?

That was easy. She'd well and truly had her fill of shocked looks that evening. Somehow the combination of the disaster with Rick *and* her infertility was just too much. Too pathetic. She didn't want the bartender's pity.

And she also hadn't told him the absolute worst bit—about what Rick had said to make her feel simultaneously all hollowed out inside and full to the brim with lead. An impossible emotion—one that surfaced far too often and one she wasn't even close to willing to share. Even with her stranger the bartender.

Wait. *Her* stranger?

It didn't matter—the important part was that with him she had opened the floodgates. Given a voice to all those swirling memories and shards of anger that she'd barely let herself think, let alone speak to anyone about. And she'd been able to because she'd never see him again.

Now she'd finished, and her sad little story was all blurted out, it was as if the bartender was coming back into focus. As she'd talked she'd paid no attention to anything except the fact that he was listening to her, and that had been all that mattered. But now she was finding it difficult to ignore the reality of him—the sharp angles of his face, his towering frame and the obvious muscled strength of his thighs so very close beside hers.

'Why did you come speed dating tonight?' he asked, his velvety voice almost a shock after what had been—if she were honest—pretty much two-hour tipsy Sophie monologue. He'd asked a few questions earlier, while she'd still felt a bit awkward, but once she'd got going—and, boy, had she—he'd just let her talk. She took a long drink of her cocktail in an attempt to keep an unwelcome surge of embarrassment at bay.

She'd have plenty of time to be mortified at all that she'd told him tomorrow. And probably for quite some time after that.

'For the usual reason, I guess—I wanted to meet someone.'

He raised his eyebrows. 'Are you sure? After all you've just told me, you don't sound like a woman who's ready to jump straight into a relationship.'

'I know,' she said, her shoulders slumping. 'It was a stupid idea. But it seemed like a good idea at the time and all that.' Her gaze fell away. 'And I really wanted to kick off my proj—'

As her brain belatedly caught up with her traitorous mouth she slammed her lips shut. Her bartender had already heard more than enough from her tonight—no need to add *totally unhinged* to her list of flaws.

'Project?' he asked.

Too late.

'It's nothing,' she said, with a brisk shake of her head. And a desperately unwanted heating of her cheeks.

Busted.

'Really?' he said, leaning forward, curiosity shining in his gaze. 'You said you're a project manager—what type of projects do you normally manage?'

'IT,' she said quickly, hoping to distract him. 'I pick up contracts for big companies. For example, my last project was for a bank in Sydney, rolling out new software. And before that I worked at a university for about six months. And…uh…'

Her words tapered off under the weight of his steady gaze.

'Did either of those projects require speed dating?' His grin was wicked.

She glared at him. Fine—so he really wanted to know?

Sophie put her glass back down on the bar with calm deliberation, then reached down for the large handbag at her

feet. Without meeting his eyes, she slid out the folded A3
piece of paper and spread it out on the bar's surface.

'I got the idea from planning my wedding,' she said. 'If
I had a plan for that, why not have one for life in general?'
She kept her gaze on the neat list of tasks and the horizon-
tal bars indicating her timelines and deadlines, bracing herself for the laughter she was sure would come. 'I've always
liked keeping lists and being organised, so this just seemed
a natural next step.'

When he remained silent, she lifted her head to find him
watching her. The absence of his teasing grin surprised her.
Instead, his lovely blue eyes seemed to look right inside her.

Great. He felt sorry for her.

What had she been thinking? She hadn't even shown her
mother the plan, knowing that she wouldn't understand. *No
one* would understand.

Especially not a handsome bartender who didn't even
know her name.

She reached out, untidily refolding the project plan. 'Forget it. It's just a stupid idea I had...'

His hand covered hers, instantly stilling her movements.
'It's not a stupid idea,' he said.

His hand was warm, much bigger than hers, his olive
complexion a stark contrast to her pale skin. Milky-white
her mother called it. Totally impractical for the Australian
climate and irritatingly fast to burn—that had always been
Sophie's opinion. But right now she liked how her skin looked
against the bartender's. Delicate—something that at five feet
ten she rarely felt.

She met his eyes. 'It does make sense,' he continued.
'You're a project manager who wants to get her life back on
track, so you're using what you know. If it works for you,
why not?'

It shocked her when her lower lip started to wobble. She'd

managed not to cry throughout the telling of her whole sad story—she was *not* going to start crying now over what was basically a glorified spreadsheet!

She swallowed, sliding her hand away from under his and immediately missing his touch. 'You haven't looked at the plan properly,' she said, pleased at her wobble-free tone. 'You may change your opinion.'

Across the top of the page the next five weeks were clearly marked, each week crammed with deliverables—many unthreateningly achievable: *Update CV. Move out of home.* Others, after tonight's speed dating failure, seemed laughably optimistic: *Find a boyfriend.* That was the worst of the lot, and of course it was a dependent task for much of the rest of the plan. Including the big one—the task that had started it all, its beribboned and embossed invitation landing in her mother's letter box like a ticking time bomb only a week earlier.

It lurked at the bottom of the task list, where she'd highlighted it in bold bloodred letters. Appropriate, she'd thought.
Attend Karen's wedding.

Three words. And such a joyous event—a close friend's marriage. And yet the prospect filled her with dread. In fact, now that she realised she'd be attending alone, she could upgrade 'dread' to 'sense of impending doom'.

'Speed dating was part of Task One?' he asked.

She nodded.

He met her eyes. '*Did* you have any luck, then? With the speed daters?'

She shook her head vehemently. 'No, not at all. I'm so far from ready for a relationship it's laughable. They were all nice guys. They deserved better than for me to waste their time.'

Sophie was almost certain she saw a subtle relaxation of the bartender's posture. Surely he couldn't be relieved? Because she didn't think talking about her ex for hours on end and then introducing her obsessive organisational skills were particularly effective flirtation techniques.

But you're not interested, remember?

'So, now do you move onto the other sub-tasks?' he asked, refocusing her on the plan and away from her misguided train of thought. *Online dating. Sign up for a new class…* His head popped up. 'Dare I ask what type of class?'

'Salsa dancing. Life drawing. Something like that.'

Now he grinned. 'Is that how you think you'll find your new boyfriend?'

She narrowed her eyes. 'Yes—and it would have worked,' she said, with total conviction. 'My projects are always a success.'

'I don't think it's possible to plot out your love life,' he said.

'I disagree,' she said simply. She'd always lived a structured life—even her adventure through South East Asia had included a carefully scheduled itinerary. And—excluding the rather massive hiccup with Rick—that life had worked for her. 'Just because you wouldn't do it that way doesn't mean it won't work.'

'How do you know I'm not a speed dating and life drawing classes kind of guy?'

It was her turn to grin. Life drawing classes for this bartender? Only if he were the model.

She ran her gaze over him. She hoped subtly. Tall, dark, handsome. Tick, tick, tick.

If he were the model at a life drawing class she certainly wouldn't be looking at any other men.

I shouldn't be looking at any *men.*

That was the point—she'd just decided she wasn't ready for a relationship. Imagining her bartender naked was not conducive to that goal. All that lovely, muscled skin…

She gave herself a mental shake.

It went without saying that he wasn't the speed dating type, either. He probably had women throwing themselves over his bar each evening—not that she was about to tell him that. And she was pretty sure he wasn't looking for a 'wife and white picket fence' future, like the men she'd met speed dating.

She snuck another glance at the bartender. He was undeniably sexy—from his short-cropped hair to his leather-clad toes.

Yeah, he was definitely the 'love 'em and leave 'em' type. Guaranteed to break a woman's heart.

'You aren't that kind of guy,' she said firmly.

'So sure?' he said, crossing his arms. 'Even though you know nothing about me?'

The reality of the past few hours of self-absorbed conversation washed over her like a bucket of ice-cold water. First the sad and sorry Rick story. Then her stupid plan.

Rapidly her icy skin was replaced with the burning heat of what felt like an all-over blush. 'I'm sorry. You must be bored out of your mind.'

He shrugged, completely unperturbed. 'You needed to talk. So I listened.'

But she realised now she wanted *him* to talk. She wanted to know more. Find out who he was, what he did outside of work—besides not going speed dating and not drawing naked people.

And wanting that was even more stupid than imagining him in the nude.

She'd talked, he'd listened, and she *did* feel better. Now she should go.

But she wanted to stay. The way he looked at her—not all the time, but sometimes—was addictive. When his gaze morphed from calm understanding to something tinged with heat and intensity, it felt…fantastic.

And it had been so incredibly long since she'd felt anything good. Anything untainted by sadness, humiliation or rejection.

It was on the tip of her tongue to offer to leave. Thank him, pay him for her many cocktails, then walk out never to see him again. Let her bartender remain just a generous and ridiculously attractive stranger.

Instead, she put down her glass and reached out her hand.

'Hi, my name's Sophie.'

'I know.' He smiled, and his gaze dropped to her chest.

She looked down, and there it was—her name in big black felt-tip capitals. 'So much for thinking I was being all mysterious.'

She ripped the forgotten name tag off and crumpled it into a ball that she dropped on the bar. Then she reached out again, determined to do this belated introduction properly.

'I'm Dan,' he said, and gripped her hand firmly.

An electric jolt flew up her arm before settling down low inside her.

A dangerous, but delicious sensation.

'Hi, Dan,' she said softly, and their eyes met. His big hand held hers just a few moments longer than absolutely necessary. 'So, if you don't think project planning is the way to meet someone, what do you suggest instead?'

Buying a woman a drink and asking if she wants to talk.

Actually saying the words had been a very near thing. Followed closely by an invitation to dinner.

But he'd stopped himself. His initial instincts had been right—very right. Sophie epitomised the type of woman he went out of his way *not* to date. She was unequivocally the long-term relationship type—with the added bonuses of recent significant emotional baggage and a project plan that was both eccentric and surprisingly endearing.

She was about as far from the type of woman he usually dated as it was possible to get.

So Dan didn't answer her question. 'I don't do relationships.'

It was a reminder to himself. No matter how lovely she was, with her mane of silky blonde hair, porcelain skin and deep pink lips, she was a woman he needed to avoid. Because the commitment that women like Sophie wanted was just not something he was capable of giving.

'Why not?'

He shot her an incredulous look. 'After your experience, you have to ask?'

'You don't want to get hurt?'

For a moment the innocent question staggered him, the words slicing through his insides like a knife.

A decade of determinedly ignored emotions simmered up inside him—but hurt certainly wasn't the most dominant. In fact it paled in comparison to the others.

Betrayal.

Loss.

Guilt.

'No,' he said. 'I just don't believe in settling down with one person.'

His tone did not invite further questioning.

But she ignored that. 'Do you want to talk about it?' she said softly. 'It's the least I can do.'

'No,' he said, more harshly than he'd intended. She'd been leaning towards him and now she straightened up abruptly, her eyes wide. 'There's nothing to talk about,' he said, more gently.

But she tilted her head, looking at him sceptically.

He ignored her assessing gaze. He'd been happy to listen

to her. After a week of stupidly long hours—the result of a bartender resigning and half his staff being struck down with the flu—it had almost been a relief to just sit still for a while and let her words flow over him.

But he wasn't about to trade stories with her.

Besides, he hadn't lied. As far as he was concerned there was *nothing* to talk about.

'I thought you said you weren't ready for a relationship?' he asked, unashamedly changing the subject.

She blinked, but nodded. 'I'm not,' she said, then gestured at the project plan, still lying on the bar in its colour-coded glory. 'And it totally stuffs up my plan.'

'What do you mean?' he said, returning his attention to the task list. He hadn't got much further than the first few lines.

Sophie didn't strike him as the kind of woman who thought she needed a man. All the tasks he'd read she could do perfectly well herself: *Find new job. Buy a car. Buy sexy underwear...*

His head popped up at that one. 'Underwear?' he asked, raising an eyebrow.

Her cheeks turned pink. 'That isn't important,' she said quickly, then tugged the plan closer to herself and stabbed her finger at the final task on the list. '*That's* the problem,' she said. 'I have to go to a *wedding*.'

She infused the word with the kind of loathing he usually associated with dental appointments and bad breakfast radio.

'Can't you just not go?' he asked.

'No!' she said. 'It's a schoolfriend's wedding. I want to go.'

He looked at her blankly.

She smiled, taking pity on him. 'It's the first wedding I've been invited to since I cancelled mine.'

He nodded as realisation dawned. 'And you don't want to go alone?'

'Exactly,' she said, the grin falling from her face. 'I was

hoping I'd meet someone new. Both as company at the wedding—someone to just hold my hand, really—and as proof I've finally gotten over Rick.'

She sighed, looking utterly defeated.

'You could still do the first one,' he said. 'The hand-holding bit. You know—ask a friend to go with you or something.'

'Yeah, I did think of that,' she said. 'Earlier, when I was doing all that contemplating at the bar.' He nodded. 'But it just seems a bit sad to take a friend. Like I can't handle it myself—even though I guess that's the whole point of all of this. A boyfriend just *looks* better.' She looked up to watch a taxi swoosh by outside—the first movement on the street in hours. 'And, trust me,' she added, 'I know how many types of wrong it is for me to be thinking like that.'

'Can you ask someone to pretend to be your boyfriend?'

He didn't know why, but finding a solution to Sophie's problem suddenly seemed vitally important. Maybe because he could picture just what she'd be like at the wedding if she went by herself—quietly strong and probably a bit distant. As she'd been when he first saw her at the bar.

She shook her head. 'Five years in Sydney means my social circle back here in Perth is minuscule—and sadly bereft of single men prepared to fake date me.'

He knew it was very wrong to be a little relieved. But he couldn't help it. He didn't like the idea of Sophie dating anyone—real or otherwise. All very irrational and caveman of him. But the truth.

'It's a pity,' she continued, leaning over and propping her chin on her hand as she studied her plan. 'It would be a great project. I could schedule in fake dates to get to know each other and figure out a back story, and there's even a barbecue being held in a few weeks for another schoolfriend's birthday that we could attend...'

He watched her, fascinated, as she ran her finger down the list, her brow furrowed in concentration. A minute later she sat up rapidly, twisting in her chair to face him directly. 'I'm going to do it,' she said, a broad smile lighting up her face. 'Thank you—it's a brilliant idea.'

Slightly stunned, it took him a moment to reply. 'I thought you just said you had no one to ask?'

'Minor problem. I've decided I'll just hire someone.'

'What?'

But her attention was back on her plan. 'Do you have a pen? I wouldn't mind updating the plan now, if you don't mind.'

'What do you mean, *hire* someone?'

'Actually, I've got a pen in my bag I think,' she said, picking it up from near her feet and plopping it onto the bar to search through. Pen in hand, she finally answered his question. 'Just like I said—I'll advertise. Or maybe try to find an actor.'

'You said you had no money?'

She scribbled out *'Find a boyfriend'* as he watched. 'I put a little aside for rental bond and a car deposit. I can use that,' she said, totally matter-of-fact.

He slid off his chair, unable to sit still. She didn't notice, her head down as she wrote furiously.

'Sophie?' he asked.

'Mmm-hmm?' she said, her attention squarely on her plan.

He reached out, meaning to still her hand as he had before, but instead he found himself rubbing his knuckles lightly—and very briefly—down her cheek, hooking a finger beneath her chin to gently tilt it upwards.

Immediately he was caught in the indigo depths of her eyes—even more compelling now he understood the sadness behind them. For a few moments they just stared at each other in silence.

Dan cleared his throat. 'Are you sure this is a good idea?' he asked.

The pen dropped with a clatter onto the bar as Sophie pulled away from him. 'What else am I meant to do?' she asked, her gaze focussed everywhere but on him. 'I don't want to go alone and I've got no one to ask.' She laughed—that terrible brittle laugh again. 'The only single man I know in Perth is *you*. And you won't do it.'

'Why are you so sure?' he said, the words out before he could capture them.

She shook her head. 'Why would you? I bet you go out with only the intimidatingly beautiful. Women who have their lives together and don't blubber all over total strangers. Women who aren't so desperate they resort to asking total strangers to be their bogus boyfriends.'

'I'll do it,' he said.

Finally she met his gaze, her eyes wide. 'I don't think that's a good idea,' she said.

If he thought he'd been stunned before, now he was totally floored. 'Pardon me?'

'You and I,' she said, pointing at Dan, then at herself, then back at him, 'would never, *ever* work.'

Even though he agreed, her rebuff was a shock to his system. Women rarely—actually, *never*—rejected him. It took him a moment to recover.

'I'd agree,' he said, 'if this were genuine. But it's not. And we're adults. We can separate the fake from the real.'

Very slowly, she nodded. 'Okay. But it's not just the wedding, you understand? If I'm going to do this, I want to do this right.'

He couldn't imagine Sophie doing anything halfway.

'But I'll make it worth your while,' she continued. 'I'll need to check my accounts, but I should be able to get the money transferred early next week—'

'I don't want your money,' he said.

Now she looked as shocked as he assumed *he* had a few minutes earlier.

'Then why would you do it?'

He had no idea.

No, that was a lie. He knew exactly why. He was being an irrational, protective caveman.

It was a mistake, and he knew it. The chemistry between them was too palpable, and the last thing Sophie needed was a guy like him—in and out of her life in a flash. A guy whose longest relationship in the last ten years had lasted just over a month.

He was not the one to give Sophie back her faith in men.

But of course that wasn't what he'd offered to do.

Now he just had to come up with an explanation for Sophie.

'It's simply business,' he said, suddenly struck by inspiration. 'I'm understaffed at the moment. If you work every Saturday night until the wedding I'll be your date.'

The bar *did* need extra help, and he always had trouble finding staff to work Saturdays. It was a legitimate business transaction.

Right.

She worried her bottom lip as she considered his words. 'That seems fair,' she said, 'as I'll need you a few hours each week for boyfriend practice.'

He liked the sound of practising.

Dan had a pretty good idea what expression he wore to warrant Sophie's cutting look, and he held up his hands in mock surrender.

But she didn't need to worry. He'd be on his very best behaviour over the next five weeks.

'Thank you,' she said with a smile. 'This is really nice of you.'

Nice was not something he associated with the idea of attending a wedding with Sophie. The opportunity to pretend to be her boyfriend—to touch her, pull her close and feel her body pressed against his…to kiss her…

Okay, maybe his *best* behaviour was pushing it. But he'd try.

'So, when are you free?' she asked. 'I'll just need to update my project plan and then we should catch up—maybe start talking about our back story?'

Already she was in project manager mode.

'How about we discuss that tomorrow…?' He glanced at his watch, not unsurprised to see it was nearly three in the morning. 'Or rather tonight?'

Her brow furrowed. 'What do you mean?'

'I mean that we'll have plenty of time to discuss our first project meeting, or whatever you want to call it, tomorrow.'

He started to collect the empty glasses, and Sophie slid off her barstool and hovered awkwardly beside him.

'Your shift starts at 5:00 p.m.,' he clarified finally. 'Wear black.'

CHAPTER THREE

The Sophie Project 2 (Project Manager: S. Morgan)
Task One: Establish ground rules

SHE was early. She always was—for everything from super-important oversize-tables-with-Sydney-Harbour-view board-room meetings to Saturday afternoon coffee with friends.

Or, as it turned out, unexpected second careers as a bar-tender. Or as a waitress—or as whatever job she was actually supposed to be doing that evening.

She'd been far too busy processing Dan's offer the night before to think to ask what exactly he'd just bartered him-self for. She suspected she'd still been a little slack-jawed with shock when he'd bundled her into a taxi at the end of the night.

No. Not night. At stupid o'clock *that morning*.

Now she sat at a white-clothed table in Dan's bar, downing a much needed cappuccino, as she waited for Dan to arrive. If the other staff members considered her sudden recruitment strange they said nothing as they carried on their business around her with barely a curious glance.

The bite of the double-shot coffee sharpened her cock-tail-fuzzed synapses, allowing more lucid consideration of Dan's offer. Which mainly focussed on the whole *Why on earth would he do this?* issue.

It sure as hell wasn't because he was desperate for a new waitress…or something.

A fancy place like the Subiaco Wine Bar didn't just hire anyone—she was sure of it. The intimidatingly efficient staff buzzing around her made that patently clear.

Another alternative job occurred to her: kitchen hand.

Oh, she hoped so. She *knew* how to wash dishes. Waiting tables? Mixing drinks? Not so much.

And she really wanted to do a good job. Desperately, even. Because she was pretty sure that Dan had offered to be her fake date for no other reason than because, under all that sexy playboy exterior, he was a bonafide knight in shining armour. Obligated to rescue all damsels in distress—even tipsy ones with project plans in their handbags.

The noble thing to do would be to let him out of it. He'd gone far above and beyond his knightly duties—listening to her babble about Rick surely met any chivalry quota.

But then she'd have to go back to her original plan and hire someone, and that prospect held zero appeal.

Plus, it would be bad for the project. If this *were* an IT project she wouldn't be knocking back the star analyst who wanted to join the team, would she?

So, to be fair, if Dan was going to sacrifice himself honourably—so to speak—for *her*, then the very least she could do was be useful. No, *better* than useful—she wanted to be the best damn temporary employee he had ever seen.

Punctuality was a valuable employee asset—so she could give herself a big tick for that. And she wore head-to-toe black clothing, as requested. Another tick.

Beyond that she was a bit lost.

At home, she'd watched online videos on waitressing skills, and beside her coffee cup she had her hastily purchased and encouragingly titled *Cocktail Bible*.

She had a feeling that her questionable memorising of

cocktail recipes and a few instructional movies wouldn't get her very far. But still she'd try:

Margarita: tequila, triple sec, lime juice, salt. Martini. Ah, yes. Lubricant of choice for sad gibberers to total strangers and, on a more positive note, unexpected purveyors of handsome wedding dates.

Gin, vermouth... But how much of each? Um...

Between The Sheets... Honestly—who thought up *that* name? White rum, brandy and...uh...

But any chance of remembering the other ingredients evaporated as Dan walked into the room. He emerged through a door at the back of the bar marked *'Staff Only'*, looking tall, and fit, and every bit as handsome as she remembered.

Dressed in loose, long shorts that hung low on his hips, a fitted T-shirt with some surf company's logo splashed across it and flip flops, he looked younger than the mid-thirties she'd guessed him to be. As he walked closer she took in the dark stubble that shadowed his jaw and implied he hadn't yet shaved that day—and then she watched him watching her.

The sweep of his eyes set her skin to tingle.

She shivered.

Damn. Ignoring her attraction to Dan was going to be more difficult than she'd expected. Unfortunately she couldn't just tick *'Forget how hot Dan* is' or *'Erase all memory of the way he looks at me'* off some imaginary emotional checklist.

She reached for the project plan as if it was a safety blanket, extracting it from amongst the pages of the *Cocktail Bible. That* was what she needed to remember: the plan. That was far more important than any five-minute fling with Dan. He'd lose interest in her in seconds, and where would that leave her?

Dateless at Karen's wedding and back to square one.

And also, she suspected, with fresh bruises all over the heart she was working so desperately to heal.

With that in mind, she stood to greet him, hand extended, fully in business mode.

'Good afternoon,' she said, making herself look him square in the eyes and training her expression—she hoped—to 'slightly remote professional'.

He raised an eyebrow. 'I think we're a bit past shaking hands,' he said.

'I don't,' she said. 'This is a business deal, so I'm treating it like one.' She straightened her shoulders and reached towards him again. 'Hi, I'm Sophie Morgan,' she said.

He wrapped his hand around hers and instantly she knew she'd made a mistake. 'A *pleasure* to meet you, Sophie,' he said, the words a rich caress down her spine. 'I'm Dan Halliday.'

This was not the brisk handshake she'd intended. It was slow and deliberate, and when Dan brushed his thumb over her knuckles and the delicate bones of the back of hand it became *tingly*. Sensation emanated from that point and grew, spreading throughout her body.

She should let go, but she couldn't. Not because he wouldn't let her, but because she seemed to have lost the ability to try.

Still holding her hand, he leant close, his breath a hot whisper beside her ear.

She froze, waiting.

'How are you today?' he said, without any sexy inflection, just quiet, genuine concern. 'Did it help last night—the talking?'

It was so unexpected. She'd anticipated—no, *braced* herself for—some flirtatious comment. But he'd surprised her.

She nodded, her throat muscles suddenly tight.

He dropped her hand, and now it was as if he was channelling a more professional version of himself. It was disconcerting, this shift from sexy to seductive to concerned to businesslike.

Who was she kidding? He'd maintained *sexy* all the way through.

She cleared her throat. 'So—uh—what will I be doing tonight?'

'Have you waitressed before?' he asked.

She shook her head. 'I worked at a fish and chip shop when I was at uni, if that helps?'

He coughed—suspiciously as if he was covering a laugh. 'Working here will be a little different.'

'I know,' she said, very aware that in this environment her Masters degree was less than useless. 'I've been doing some research,' she continued, gesturing at the book propped open on the table. 'Making cocktails, how to wait tables—that sort of thing.'

He smiled. 'You *are* always organised, aren't you?'

'I try,' she said. 'Although it was hard to prepare when I didn't know what I'd be doing. Guess I should have focussed on waitressing, then?'

Dan nodded. 'Yeah. We need an extra person on the floor tonight.'

'I'll do my best.'

They stood in awkward silence for a moment, before Dan said gruffly, 'I'll ask Kate to come show you the ropes. Any questions—ask her. I'll be behind the bar.'

With a nod, he walked over to a small, dark-haired woman whom she assumed to be Kate—the lucky lady with the task of transforming Sophie Morgan, Project Manager, into Sophie Morgan, Waitress.

Waitressing. Not as reassuringly straightforward as washing dishes—although it was a relief to stop worrying about martinis, Caprioskas and Fuzzy Navels, or the final ingredient of Between The Sheets.

She couldn't stop herself running her eyes over the impressive width of Dan's shoulders as he spoke to Kate, his back to Sophie. Or letting her gaze dip lower, admiring *all* of his rear view. *Geez.* She even found the dark hair sprinkling his calves attractive.

But at least she'd solved the mystery of that cocktail's name.

Yep, she'd bet a woman had named it.

Right after meeting a man like Dan Halliday.

Much earlier that day—like at four in the morning—Dan had walked the short distance from the bar to his townhouse, reassuring himself that he *hadn't* just made a huge mistake.

With the whisper of a breeze ruffling the leaves along his tree-lined street the only accompaniment to the dull echo of his boots on the bitumen, he'd done his best to justify his actions.

Sophie was hurting. He felt sorry for her. He was helping her out.

End of story.

For a while he'd believed that, too. He'd been comfortable in that knowledge all day.

As he'd swum his regular laps along Cottesloe Beach he'd even smugly considered the brilliance of the business side of the arrangement. A few hours of his time for a free employee—excellent!

Of course seeing Sophie again, her black clothes highlighting the paleness of her skin and her deep golden hair, had reminded him of his less altruistic reasons.

Touching her had only underlined them.

He could spin it any way he wanted, but the truth was he *liked* Sophie. He liked that she was smart, he liked that she was beautiful—he even liked her project plan.

What he *didn't* like was that some moron had damaged her. He didn't like that at all.

So he could tell himself he was just being a nice guy, but it was more than that. He'd wanted to see her again.

Actually, he wanted more than that. Quite simply, he wanted *her*.

And not in the happy-ever-after way that Sophie needed. In a much more primal, 'twisted sheets and tangled naked limbs' kind of way.

But that would be a very bad idea.

If he stuck to the plan they'd be fine. Sophie would get her wedding date, he'd get an extra employee—and surely it wouldn't take long for the heat between them to cool? Then the arrangement would be purely business. Just as he'd told her it was.

Yes. That was it. He'd just wait it out. Sophie would be out of his life in five weeks, and he could go back to dating more suitable women.

All he had to do was keep his hands off Sophie and it would work out fine.

With that in mind, he remained resolutely professional whenever she came to the bar to collect drinks, treating her exactly the same as he did his other employees.

If—very occasionally—he watched her take an order, or walk away from the bar, while admiring the dramatic curve of her waist and hips in a very non-employer/employee appropriate kind of way—well, it couldn't be helped.

It was while he talked to a regular customer, rattling a cocktail shaker as they spoke, that he heard the unmistakeable crash and smash of many plates hitting the ground.

He looked over to see Sophie, standing smack bang in the centre of the restaurant part of the bar, the remnants of some unfortunate customer's dinner dumped at her feet. For a second it was silent as diners and staff turned to look at her as one.

Her face was totally white as she stared at the mess. Then she lifted her gaze—straight to him. As she did, the murmur of conversation and the clink of cutlery clicked back into place and the noise that had disturbed them was forgotten.

'I'm really sorry,' she said—or maybe just mouthed. She was too far away for him to hear. He smiled—he hoped re-assuringly—but she still looked totally stricken.

He quickly poured the cocktail, then headed over to Sophie, who had knelt down to collect the pieces of broken crockery.

He squatted beside her, dropping the tray he'd carried from the bar onto the floor and started piling pieces of shiny white porcelain onto it.

'I'm sorry,' she said quietly. 'I know I'm sucking at this.'

'Don't stress,' he said. 'Everyone makes mistakes when they're new. You look to be doing fine to me.'

He reached across her to grab the last section of broken plate, causing their shoulders to bump gently together.

She twisted to look at him. 'You really think that? I keep forgetting the specials, and I have a bad feeling I've served at least one person the wrong meal. Or the wrong drink.'

'I'm sure you haven't,' he said. Miss Organisation wasn't about to make that type of mistake. 'And besides, I didn't expect perfection.'

She gave a little huff of frustration. 'But I *want* to be really good at this, you know? To make this whole wedding date thing a fair deal. And all I've managed to do is break your plates and ruin someone's dinner.'

'Hey,' he said, and their shoulders touched again as he shifted his weight. 'I'm happy with the deal.'

She narrowed her eyes. 'Why? What are you getting out of it other than a dodgy waitress?'

It was terrible timing, but his gaze dropped—completely without his permission—to her lips.

She went completely still.

And then her eyes widened, before travelling south, too.

Really? Was he thinking about kissing Sophie surrounded by splattered risotto and chilli mussels and in a room full of people?

And it had been less than an hour since his decision to keep his distance. Pathetic.

He needed to do better than this.

Without a word he stood and forced himself back into professional bar-owner/manager mode—mollifying the intended recipients of the ruined dinner with a free meal, organising a kitchen hand and a mop to fix the rest of the mess, and then going back behind the safety of the bar, pouring wine and mixing cocktails with one hundred percent concentration.

He'd treat Sophie just as the employee she was. Nothing more.

It was a pity he couldn't quite make himself believe that.

Sophie stood patiently as the chef made his finishing touches to the three desserts she was awaiting for Table Two. The desserts were in the same style as the rest of the menu—simple, unpretentious and delicious. Or at least she assumed delicious, given the very little food left on the plates she'd been clearing all night. She hadn't had a chance to eat yet. Or stand still. Or talk. Or think.

She couldn't remember the last time she'd felt so completely exhausted or so completely incompetent.

Or so completely flustered?

She'd felt Dan's eyes on her—a constant tingling awareness that had scrambled her brain at the most inopportune moments. Like when customers were ordering their meals.

Or when she was—possibly a bit too optimistically—carrying too many plates at once.

She'd just about convinced herself that his attention was that of a concerned bar-owner—to the point of cultivating a little righteous frustration that it was *his* fault she kept flubbing the specials and had discovered her previously dormant clumsiness.

But then there'd been those few minutes when they'd knelt side by side on the floor, and any logical explanation for why he'd been looking at her had gone right out of the window. She'd seen the heat in his eyes—and known what it meant.

He'd been thinking about kissing her.

And just for a moment—maybe even less than that—a *millisecond*—she'd been thinking the same thing.

Not good.

Finally the chef finished adding chocolate sauce flourishes to the individual baked cheesecakes. She rocked side to side on her aching feet, trying to figure out how to handle this.

Was that why Dan had agreed to be part of her project? Did he think she was up for a no-strings-attached fling? Maybe he wasn't quite the magnanimous knight in shining armour she'd cast him as.

She would almost not blame him, if that *was* what he planned. She was sure he knew that she was attracted to him. She had, after all, basically turned into a puddle of lust when he'd simply shaken her hand.

But she'd already decided that starting something with Dan was a bad idea, and she wasn't about to be convinced otherwise. Despite the actions of her traitorous hormones.

The chef pushed the finished desserts plates forward for her, and she carefully arranged them—two plates on one arm, one on the other—just as Kate had shown her. Another waitress watched with obvious trepidation.

'You sure you've got those?' she asked, but Sophie wasn't worried.

This time she was determined to deliver the food unscathed—through pure willpower alone if necessary.

With a reassuring smile she headed for the single remaining occupied table and managed to serve all three cheesecakes with barely a wobbly moment.

Triumphant, she walked back to the bar rather than the kitchen. She knew she should be wiping down tables, or some other end-of-the-night, wannabe-best-employee-ever task, but instead she went to Dan. They needed to sort this out.

He was wiping down the counter top, but he glanced up as she approached. He'd shaved earlier, after his shower, but she didn't even get to miss his sexy stubble as he easily looked just as good clean-shaven.

But of course his perpetual state of gorgeousness would *not* cause her to waver in her decision. If he'd really only agreed to be her wedding date to get her into bed then she needed to end this now.

'I bet you didn't think you'd be working here this time yesterday,' he said.

Sophie's eyes darted to the clock above the bar. It had been twenty-four hours since she'd accepted Dan's offer to talk. It felt a million years ago.

'No, definitely not.' Without her asking, Dan poured a glass of water and put it on a coaster in front of her. 'Thank you,' she said.

She watched him over the rim of her glass as she drank and he polished yet more stemware. She needed to just come out and say it.

'How long ago did you open the bar?' She figured she'd work her way up to the 'if you're just in this for sex you're out of luck' thing.

'Ten years ago,' he said. 'I bought the other bar five years later.'

'Other bar?'

Dan nodded, putting the last glass away and then hanging the cloth on a bar beneath the sink. 'Yeah, in Fremantle. It's almost twice as big as this place.'

She was impressed. This bar wasn't exactly small. 'You must have been pretty young when you bought this place, then?'

'Twenty-five,' he said, then grinned. 'What is this? Twenty questions?'

She felt her cheeks heat. 'I'm just curious,' she said. 'You know so much about me, and I know nothing about you.'

Also, every minute she spent in his company further convinced her that she'd gone way off track with her theory. Even as they spoke two young women perched at the opposite end of the bar were watching Dan with undisguised interest. And how could she have forgotten his easy banter with customers all evening? Women hung off his every word. And she had thought Dan was having her work in his bar, pretending to be dating her, just to get *her* into bed? *Sophie Morgan?* When he could have his pick of anyone?

Now it seemed ludicrous. Dan didn't need to jump through hoops to get sex. He probably just needed to shoot a smouldering look in some unsuspecting girl's direction.

'What do you want to know?' he asked.

Who are you? Ruthless player or gallant knight?

'Have you always wanted to own bars?' she asked instead.

'No,' he said. 'I used to be a lawyer.'

'Really?' she said, surprised. She couldn't imagine Dan cooped up behind a desk all day.

He laughed, obviously able to see what she was thinking. 'I know. But it's true—and for a while I loved it.'

'What changed?'

His gaze slid away from hers, but she didn't miss his fleeting grimace. 'Nothing,' he said, 'It was just time for a change.'

She didn't believe him. His expression was reminiscent of one from the previous night—when she'd made the mistake of asking if he was scared of being hurt.

Her every instinct was to push—to ask him again and find out what—or rather *who*—had made Dan turn his life upside down.

But before she had a chance the girls at the end of the bar gestured to get his attention and he walked over.

The final table had finished their desserts, and so she'd lost her chance to ask more questions—although she was certain he wouldn't have been forthcoming. His shuttered expression was as good as a 'Keep Out' sign.

By the time she'd cleared the table, and the customers had paid their bill and left, the other staff had started to filter out of the kitchen, heading for the door and throwing goodbyes over their shoulders. The same cleaner from last evening swept the dining area, and she smiled at him as she headed back to the now empty bar. If he was surprised she'd been transformed from customer to employee he didn't show it.

Sophie picked up the coasters and empty glasses the young women who'd been eyeing Dan had left behind. The scrawled name and phone number on one of the coasters didn't surprise her one little bit.

See! He can have anyone.

Dan was counting the money from the till when she walked behind the bar and dropped the coaster on the counter beside him.

'I think this is for you,' she said, in what was supposed to be a casual tone but instead ended up stiff and awkward. She swallowed, hoping he hadn't noticed.

No such luck.

He grinned and raised an eyebrow. 'You disapprove?'

She shook her head. 'Of course not!' Again, not the relaxed, breezy tone she'd hoped for. 'Why would I? It's none of my business.'

None at all.

She stacked the empty wine glasses into the dishwasher tray with a little more force than necessary.

What was wrong with her?

Out of the corner of the eye she saw him slip the coaster into his pocket. She clenched her teeth. Then realised what she was doing and relaxed her jaw. Took a deep breath.

'I'd like to organise our first project meeting,' she said.

There. That was better.

'Sure,' he said. 'Just tell me when and where.'

'Tuesday—at whatever time suits you,' she said. She was the unemployed one, after all. Then she named a nearby café she thought would be suitable.

'How about you meet me down at Cottesloe Beach?' he said. 'I swim laps most afternoons, and it's supposed to be hot this week. You could come for a swim, too.'

'No!' she said. Dan with his shirt off and all those rippling muscles—she was sure he had them—and her in a three-year-old faded bikini and deathly white skin? *No way.*

He shrugged. 'Just a suggestion.'

'I just want to keep things professional,' she said.

'I suggested a swim on a hot day,' he said. 'Not rolling around together on the sand.'

Not an image she needed.

He laughed at her shocked expression.

'Calm down, Sophie,' he said. 'I get it. You want to stick to the plan.'

She swallowed. 'Yes, I do. This is no different to one of my work projects. It's a professional arrangement—each of us trading our services. No funny business involved.'

'Funny business?' he said with a laugh. 'What are you? One hundred years old?'

She glared at him. 'You know what I mean.'

He held his hand to his heart. 'I solemnly swear that I, Dan Halliday, will not ravish Sophie Morgan.'

When he put it that way, she felt completely ridiculous.

'I'm sure you'll be able to restrain yourself,' she said dryly.

'I will,' he said, than added mournfully, 'somehow…'

'Stop it!' she said, reaching out without thinking to shove him gently. 'I just think it's easier if we know where we stand. Before—when I dropped the plates…' The words trailed off and she blushed as Dan caught her gaze. He knew exactly what she was talking about.

'It's okay. I agree with you. You and I would never work.'

They were the same words she'd used, but somehow when Dan said them they made her feel a little empty inside.

She *really* needed to pull herself together.

'That's good,' she said simply. And it was. She just needed to keep reminding herself of that.

'But more seriously,' he said, looking at her without humour in his gaze, 'if we're going to pull this off we'll need to put on a show for people. Touch, hold hands, kiss—that sort of stuff.'

She nodded slowly. 'I guess. But maybe we should have some ground rules. Just so neither of us gets the wrong idea.'

He reached out, and she froze as he tucked a loose lock of hair behind her ear. He leant close. 'So this would be okay, then?' he said, his voice deep and seductive. 'Touching you like this?'

She took a step back. 'There was no need for the demonstration, but yes,' she said, a little unevenly. 'And definitely no kissing,' she said firmly.

She had a terrible feeling that if Dan kissed her she'd find it impossible to stop at one.

'I don't think that'll work,' he said. 'We're supposed to be a couple in love.'

'Fine,' she conceded. 'But only on the cheek.'

He shrugged. 'Cheeks only it is. Whatever you want, Sophie.'

Ah, but this wasn't about what she *wanted* from Dan. Every traitorous bone in her body *wanted* Dan.

But what she *needed* was a 'no fuss' date to Karen's wedding. That was all.

In keeping with their reaffirmed arrangement, Dan was brisk and businesslike as he finished closing the bar for the evening. Lights finally switched off, and everything locked up, he walked her across the tiny, crunchy-gravelled car park to her mum's faded red hatchback.

She unlocked the door, but stopped before she opened it, turning to look up at Dan.

'Thank you for doing this,' she said softly.

He shrugged. 'I just need some extra help at the bar.'

Yes. That was all it was. Time to stop over-analysing and searching for ulterior motives. He wasn't some dastardly playboy hell-bent on seduction, and neither was he her own personal knight in shining armour.

He was just a guy helping her out. And she was helping *him* out. That was it. The end.

She opened the door and slid into the car, then reached out to pull the door closed—only to have the movement blocked by Dan's broad shoulders as he leant towards her.

'You did great tonight,' he said, his voice a smooth whisper against her ear.

And then his lips touched her cheek, instantaneously soft and firm.

Perfect. But in a split second his touch was gone, and he was unfolding himself back to his full height.

She couldn't stop her hand creeping up to touch her face where he'd kissed her.

'Thought I'd better try out this cheek-kissing thing,' he said, his tone only a little louder than before. 'Get some practice in. I don't know about you, but I think that one was pretty good.'

She nodded, her ability to form coherent words deserting her.

'Good,' he said again.

A minute or two later, just when she thought he was about to lean down and kiss her again, he turned and walked away.

CHAPTER FOUR

The Sophie Project 2.0 (Project Manager: S. Morgan)
Task Two: Planning Meeting No. 1 Rewrite Plan

'SERIOUSLY, Sophie, a suit?'

Dan stopped a few metres away from the café table, running his eyes appreciatively along the fitted lines of Sophie's light grey skirt and baby pink blouse. At least she'd hung her jacket on the back of her chair as a small concession to the warm November afternoon.

She looked up from her laptop. 'I've been meeting with some contacts in the city, as unfortunately I need to get a job at some point. This,' she said, casually pointing down at her clothes, 'is not for you.'

Maybe not, but he could still enjoy the view.

'So we're not going all formal and hand-shaking again, then?' he asked, raising his eyebrows.

'No,' she said, her lovely blue eyes sparkling but direct. 'But we're still keeping this one hundred percent professional, right?'

'I don't think we could've been any clearer than in our last conversation,' he said wryly.

That was, of course, if you ignored his total lapse of judgement in the car park. That kiss had come from nowhere, minutes after he'd silently berated himself for teasing her when she'd so awkwardly attempted to establish her 'ground rules'. Why, when he agreed with her, had he teased her?

And why, when he knew it was wrong, had he kissed her?

He took the seat across from her, dropping his backpack at his feet—he'd come straight from the beach—and his sunglasses onto the table. They were at the back of the café, surrounded by empty tables—a stark contrast to the busy alfresco area outside. All those sensible people were basking in the sea breeze, icy cold drinks in hand.

Instead he'd got a table full of project plans, checklists and…his own file.

He reached for the black folder with some trepidation. His name was printed clearly on the spine. 'Uh, Sophie— what's this?'

'That's your project file. I thought it would be easier if I put everything together for you.' She grinned. 'It's pretty cool, huh?'

He opened it and flicked through the section dividers: *Our History, About Sophie, About Dan, Task Schedule* and, of course, *Project Plan.*

The *About Sophie* section documented her basic information: date of birth, the schools she'd attended, her parents' names—that sort of thing—while all the others remained blank.

'You don't think this is a little excessive?' he asked.

'Probably,' she said, shrugging unapologetically. 'But hey, if you're going to do something, might as well do it right.'

He didn't even know why he was surprised—the file was pure Sophie. He flipped back to her section, reading the first page with interest.

'I thought a lady never revealed her age,' he said. She was twenty-nine—six years younger than him.

'In this instance it's essential,' she said, in what he assumed was her sensible project manager voice. 'You never know what we're going to get asked at the wedding, or at the barbecue. Given we're—apparently—madly in love, we'll be expected to know that type of stuff.'

'Is that the barbecue you mentioned the other night?' he asked.

'Yeah,' she said. 'It's in the project plan.' She pushed his file aside and spread the plan in front of him. It was large enough that she'd needed to tape several sheets of paper together for it to fit. She ran her finger three quarters down the page. 'See? There. A good friend from school is having it for her birthday. It's perfect, as Karen and her fiancé will be there too, plus a lot of the guests.'

'Right.' He nodded, scanning the page. He saw that each task was marked with pink for Sophie, or blue for him. There were a *lot* of blue tasks. Actually, nearly all of them.

He checked all the pink tasks. 'What happened to underwear shopping?' he asked.

She narrowed her eyes. 'I've got two versions of the plan. Yours is a condensed version, just with the parts from *The Boyfriend Plan.*'

For a moment he just stared at her.

'The whole thing I'm calling *The Sophie Project*,' she clarified, 'because that's what it is. But I'm calling your bit *The Boyfriend Plan* to keep it all straight in my head.' She smiled at him. 'I know what you're thinking, but I promise I'm not totally insane,' she said. 'Just organised.'

'I'll take your word for it.'

'Anyway,' she hurried on, 'it'll make more sense when I walk you through it. But first—here.' She passed him a pen. He half expected it to be emblazoned with his name, but thankfully it wasn't. 'Can you fill out this questionnaire?'

She passed him a few typewritten sheets of paper that matched the pages he'd seen in her file. But all the details were blank. There was space for him to answer each question—everything from where he'd been born through to the name of his last girlfriend.

As Sophie returned to typing away on her laptop, he began to answer the questions.

Siblings? None.

Cultural background? Australian/Croatian.

Parents/Grandparents? One set of each. His father's parents long dead; his mother's Croatian parents still going strong.

Ever married? His hand stilled.

He read the next question. *Any children?*

He put the pen aside and slid the questionnaire into the folder. 'I'll finish this later,' he said.

She looked up, surprised. 'Are you sure you can't do it now? We need to start studying each other's backgrounds right away.' She paused, then added, 'Actually, I just like seeing "100% Complete" beside as many items as possible. It's compulsive—what can I say?'

She grinned, but he didn't smile back.

'I have an appointment after this. I don't have much time.'

Her eyebrows drew together. 'I thought you said this was your day off?'

'Something came up,' he said firmly. He didn't like lying to her, but he wasn't about to fill out the questionnaire, either.

'Oh,' she said, frowning. 'Well…uh…let's go through the project plan instead.'

She stood, dragging her chair beside his so they could both look at the plan the right way up.

She reached across him to grab her pen, close enough that he could smell the coconut scent of her hair. It was distracting, having her so close. Annoyingly so.

Having her close heated his skin, disrupted his thoughts, messed with his head. It reminded him of why he'd kissed her in the car park. It reminded him of why he wished that sanity hadn't prevailed and he'd kissed her on the mouth instead of walking away.

It reminded him of why, when he'd pulled that coaster out of his pocket, he'd thrown it away rather than calling the woman as he'd intended.

Her knee knocked against his. 'Sorry,' she said, turning her head as she spoke.

She gasped as she realised how close they now were—their foreheads, noses, *lips* mere centimetres apart.

Within seconds she'd shoved her chair backwards and retreated to the other side of the table. 'It'll be easier if I show you from here,' she said. 'More room.'

'Good idea,' he said, and it was. An excellent idea. Space helped neutralise the sparks between them enough that Dan could actually pay attention to what she was saying, rather than imagining how good she'd look in that sexy underwear she was planning on buying.

And paying attention was clearly a *very* important thing to do, once he began to register what some of the tasks assigned to him actually were.

'Wait,' he said, interrupting her. 'Did you just say *clothes shopping*?'

'Yes,' she said patiently. 'For the wedding. I'll buy you a suit.'

'I have plenty of suits,' he said, appalled. 'I don't take women out for dinner or go to industry functions in board shorts and flip flops.' As he was currently wearing. 'Don't worry, I won't embarrass you.'

'Oh, I didn't mean that!' she said, blushing a deep red. 'Not at all. You always look great.'

He raised his eyebrows. 'You think so?'

She tilted her head, widening her eyes innocently. 'What? You didn't notice all the women swooning in your wake today?'

He grinned. 'Sadly, no.'

'I'd imagine it must get tiresome, wading through the resulting piles of besotted women.'

He laughed out loud. 'Sweetheart, you have no idea.'

Her gaze shifted as she scanned his face. He could as good as see little cogs turning as her brain ticked over. 'It must be unusual for you, having a woman uninterested in you.'

Uninterested in how little he could offer her, definitely. She was lying to herself if she pretended there was no chemistry between them.

You deserve better than a guy like me.

He said nothing.

Sophie gave a little shake of her head as she refocussed on her project. 'Anyway. The clothes shopping was just about getting the look I want. The wedding date is like the final project deliverable. I want it to be perfect.'

'You do know I'm not a doll you get to play dress-up with? Just tell me what colour your dress is and I'll wear something that won't clash. Easy.'

'But—'

'No clothes shopping,' he said.

She explored his face for a few moments, as if she was gauging whether to argue further. 'Fine,' she said finally, reluctantly. 'I'll update the plan.'

Over the next half an hour Sophie walked him through the task lists—which mostly seemed to consist of planning meetings to map out their back story and quiz each other on pertinent facts about their life histories. Not exactly thrilling stuff.

'So that's it?' he asked, when Sophie finally reached the end. 'Coffee meetings and quizzes for the next five weeks, one barbecue and one wedding?'

'Yes,' she said.

'It's a good plan…'

'But...?' Sophie asked.

'I think you're going about it the wrong way.'

She crossed her arms defensively. 'How do you mean? I spent hours working on this. I can't think of any better way to prepare.'

'I think that's the problem,' he said. 'You've got a meeting to plan how we met, and then another meeting for our first date, plus all those quizzes so we can get to know each other. All that effort and time spent *preparing*, when it would be a heck of a lot easier to just *do* it.'

'Do what?'

'Date,' he said. 'And before you start over-reacting, not for real. Fake date. Just like a real date—where you have dinner, find out about each other—with the added bonus that we're actually *experiencing* the date we're supposed to have had.'

'I guess then it wouldn't feel like such a lie,' she said quietly. 'That's good. That's really the only flaw in the plan... the having to lie bit.' She chewed on her bottom lip. 'But it would still be all make-believe, yeah?'

'Yes,' he said. 'But about a hundred times more enjoyable than learning each other's life history by rote.'

'Hmm,' she said, a blond-ponytailed picture of scepticism. 'But what if we don't cover everything in the file?'

'Why do we have to? Can't we just say we met speed dating last weekend, then started dating—and get to know each other like normal people?'

'I guess...' she said, her attention on the pen she twirled around and around with her fingers. 'But wouldn't you rather spend your evenings with women you're *actually* dating?'

'I'll squeeze you in,' he said.

'You really don't have to. I'm happy just to keep meeting during the day—'

'Sophie, I was *joking*. Despite your flattering assessment

of my appeal to women, I'm not seeing anyone at the moment. I'm all yours…so to speak. Until the wedding.'

She nodded slowly. Then rotated the project plan so it faced her again. He watched as she scanned the tasks, her brow knitted in concentration.

'This could work,' she said after a few minutes. She crossed out one of the planning meetings. Then another. 'Actually,' she said, her voice warming with enthusiasm, 'it's actually a really efficient way of doing this. Streamlines the whole project. I like it.'

'Good,' he said as he stood, hefting his backpack over his shoulder. 'I'll pick you up on Friday at eight, then.'

'Where are we going?'

'It's our first date—it's a surprise.'

She shook her head. 'No, I really don't like surprises. I like to be—'

'Prepared?' he said.

'Exactly!' She gave him a relieved smile.

But then, for no other reason than he liked seeing perfectly coiffed, perfectly organised Sophie Morgan rattled, he said, 'I know. But bad luck. I'll see you Friday.'

CHAPTER FIVE

The Sophie Project 2.1 (Project Manager: S. Morgan)
Task Three: The First Date

SOPHIE paced from one end of her mother's living room to the other, her heels loud on the half-century-old jarrah floorboards.

'That won't make him get here faster, you know,' her mother said, curled up in the corner of the beige leather sofa with the paperback she was pretending to read on her lap.

'I don't *want* him to get here faster,' Sophie replied, making herself turn away from the window and the view of the street it offered.

'Whatever you say, darling,' her mother said, with an irritatingly wise nod.

Sophie put her hands on her hips. Her fingers slid against the snug-fitting silky fabric of her dress—a dress that might or might not be suitable for her mystery date destination.

'*Mum*, you know what I'm like. I'm fidgety because I don't know where I'm going—and I *hate* that. It's got nothing to do with Dan.' When her mother replied by raising one of her perfectly manicured eyebrows, Sophie huffed in frustration. 'You're not being at all subtle, you know—doing the whole *I'll just happen to be reading on the couch next to the front door when he arrives* thing. I see right through you.'

Her mother sniffed. 'As if I'd miss *this*! It isn't every day you get to meet your daughter's fake boyfriend.'

Unfortunately telling her mother about the plan had been unavoidable. Partly because she could come up with no valid explanation for her sudden transformation from virtual recluse to arriving home in the silly hours of the morning, but mainly because she hated lying to her mum. Her mother might be equal parts nosy and opinionated, but she was also an unquestionably awesome parent. Bringing Sophie and her sister up by herself could never have been easy—and then when years of hospital stays were thrown into the mix…

'You need to remember that,' Sophie said, making herself sit beside her mother and ignore the hum of tension resonating through her body—or at least try to. 'The fake bit. It's not real. It's totally platonic.' Up went her mother's eyebrow again, so she added, 'Look, we're not even *attracted* to each other.'

That outright lie managed to drop her unflappable mother's jaw.

'Well, maybe a little bit,' she conceded. Sometimes she was sure her cheek still burned from his kiss. 'But nothing's going to happen. We both agree.'

With a sigh, her mum scooted closer and wrapped an arm around Sophie's shoulder. 'Are you sure you're ready for this, hon?'

Her attention steadfast on the fastest of the super-kitsch porcelain ducks that flew across the pale yellow wall, she said, tone firm, 'I just said—it's *fake*.'

'Let's for argument's sake imagine it isn't.'

The urge to leap up from the cocooning softness of the leather couch and restart her pacing was near impossible to suppress. But instead she made herself turn to face her mother.

'I'm not ready to jump into something new,' she said.

'That's why I'm doing this rather than speed dating, or on-line dating, or however else I'd been planning to find a *real* boyfriend. Getting a real boyfriend for Karen's wedding was the dumb idea. *This* is the sensible one.'

A rather liberal definition of 'sensible', for sure. More sensible than expecting to let go of all her hurt and anger and sorrow and fall in love conveniently in time for the wedding anyway.

'You don't *need* a date for the wedding, you know.'

It wasn't the first time her mum had pointed out this un-arguable truth.

Of course she didn't need a date for the wedding. Every strong, independent bone in her body knew that—in fact *rebelled* against the idea that she should even consider a wedding date a necessity.

So she didn't *need* a wedding date.

But—and she hated this reality—she *wanted* one. Badly. Desperately, even.

A short seven months earlier she'd attended a wedding with Rick. Of course she'd had not even the tiniest inkling that anything was up, or that her perfectly constructed life was about to dissolve before her eyes. No, *instead* she'd had a wonderful evening, loving both the utter romance of the wedding and the opportunity for her brain to observe, analyse and file away snippets and ideas for her own wedding. She'd even taken a few notes in a tiny notepad hastily stuffed inside her clutch, for goodness' sake!

And it *had* been beautiful, that wedding. More than once, with an excited squeeze of his arm or a touch on his thigh at dinner, she'd whispered to Rick, 'The next wedding we go to will be ours!'

The next wedding she was going to would be Karen's.

That wasn't how it was supposed to be.

The unmistakable slap of leather shoes on her mother's

authentic 1960s cement front porch, followed shortly thereafter by a deliberate knock on the door, saved Sophie from attempting to explain.

With yet another raised eyebrow and a long look that Sophie could only interpret to mean *Be careful* or possibly *Don't do anything stupid*, her mother curled back into the corner of the sofa. Sophie smoothed her hands down the midnight-blue fabric that covered her thighs and with a deep breath channelled her best impersonation of a calm, totally-has-her-stuff-together woman.

Half believing it herself, she walked to the door and twisted the handle.

You're nervous because you don't know where you're going. You're anxious because of the upcoming wedding.

The butterflies are not because Dan is standing behind the door.

She swung the door open.

Dan stood there, tall and dark, his face a kaleidoscope of shadows thrown by the sensor light that had flickered on behind him.

'Hey,' he said.

He wore dark grey trousers and a crisp white shirt, no tie—a whole other type of handsome from bartender Dan or board shorts Dan. She liked those too, but this version was a particular favourite. Maybe because she liked the contrast of his stark white shirt against the olive skin the two unfastened buttons at his collar revealed. Or the unbidden question it raised—was he that colour all over?

Or maybe it was because she knew he was about to whisk her away on a date—just the two of them, alone together.

No. Wait. *What?*

Unbelievable. One glance at Dan and she'd forgotten this was a facsimile of a date. Fluttering tummy butterflies and romantic notions had no place here.

Flustered, and realising she'd been standing dumbstruck and silent for far too long, she said the first thing that occurred to her.

'You look great.'

Not ideal, but at least she'd managed to form words. Unfortunately now she had to scramble to provide adequate justification. 'I mean, I appreciate that you made an effort—like this is a *real* date. Which it *isn't*, of course. I know that. But I guess it's possible we could bump into someone I know, or maybe someone would—'

'Sophie?' he said, cutting her off. 'I get it. And just for the record...?'

She nodded, waiting as his gaze swept over her, leaving a wave of tingling sensation in its wake.

He cleared his throat. 'You look way better than great.'

Five minutes later Sophie was settling into the leather passenger seat of Dan's jet-black, low-slung, two-door sports sedan. The car suited him—darkly attractive and effortlessly sexy.

But totally impractical and completely unsuitable in the long-term.

She couldn't forget that.

'Your mum's nice,' he said, pulling away from the kerb. 'No probing questions or veiled threats against your honour. Always a plus when meeting the parents.'

Sophie gave an inelegant snort of laughter. 'And how often do you bother to meet a girl's parents, exactly?'

He nodded. 'Fair point. But believe it or not, when I was much younger and sillier, I may have been known to do so— once or twice.'

There it was again, a flash of something—anger? Regret?—across his face. 'Who were these lucky ladies who persuaded you to do such a thing?'

He lips quirked up in a grin as he saw right through her.

'Nice try. But past girlfriends aren't a standard first date topic of conversation, are they?'

Sophie sighed. 'But this *isn't* a real date.'

'It isn't one of your project planning meetings in disguise, either. Let's just go with the flow. See where the night takes us.'

She didn't like the sound of that. Or rather, she did—which was the problem.

'Where are we going?'

She was rewarded for that question with a deliberately raised eyebrow. 'The flow, remember?'

She crossed her arms, jiggling her legs in frustration. The action slid her dress further apart from her knees. Why had it never seemed too short until she slid into Dan's car?

With a subtle smoothing of the fabric, she attempted to hide a gentle tug to pull it lower before Dan noticed.

No such luck. She felt his eyes on her the moment his attention flicked momentarily from the road. She shouldn't be surprised—men always seemed to have a special radar for displays of naked flesh.

She also shouldn't have been surprised when her skin goosepimpled beneath his gaze. Annoyed at herself, definitely, but not surprised. She should be used to the way her body responded to Dan. And by now she should be a heck of a lot better at ignoring it.

'Are you close to your parents?' she asked, both to say something and because she wanted to know.

Dan glanced at her across the centre console. 'Are you asking for your questionnaire?'

'No,' she said, shaking her head. That hadn't even occurred to her. 'You met my mum, and I'm curious about yours. And your dad too, of course.'

Her own father had walked out long before she was old enough to remember him.

'Well,' he said, 'I have one of each. Mum is tall, Croatian, bossy and a fantastic cook, while Dad is taller, a fourth generation Aussie, and loves to eat her food. That's about it.'

'What do they do?'

'Enjoy the leisurely life of the retired and lament my early exit from the family profession and my rejection of anything resembling settling down.'

That sentence was easily the most candid Dan had uttered since she'd met him.

'They were lawyers too?' she asked.

He nodded. 'But I think that's enough sharing of family history for a first date, don't you?'

She didn't miss the infinitesimal tightness of his voice, and it was enough to silence the many questions teetering at the tip of her tongue. She knew Dan well enough now to see she needed to quit when she was ahead.

'Fine, then—what should we talk about instead?'

'Normal first date stuff. Like what are your hobbies?'

'Other than spreadsheets?'

He grinned. 'Yes, other than spreadsheets.'

'Well, in my spare time,' she said, deadpan, 'I like to make lists…'

Dan laughed. 'I just bet you do.'

They ended up at one of Perth's best fine dining restaurants—a tiny, exclusive venue nestled behind the dunes of Cottesloe Beach.

So, yes, she was appropriately dressed—which was a huge relief.

Actually, no. Not really.

As they pulled into the restaurant's car park and their destination became clear, that tight coil of tension in her belly should have instantly loosened. Dan hadn't planned an evening skydiving, or any other ridiculous date possibility that she'd considered.

But it didn't. She felt just as wound up, and not one of those darn tummy butterflies had reduced its fluttering.

They continued their flapping as Dan asked the sommelier for wine recommendations. 'Sophie doesn't like red,' he said.

Wines ordered, and sommelier on his way, Sophie looked at him with surprise. 'How did you know that?' she asked.

'I've been reading your file.'

She narrowed her eyes. 'I didn't think you believed in the file. Aren't we supposed to be getting to know each other "like normal people"?'

'Normal people don't dot point their life stories into two pages or less.' He shrugged. 'Of course I read it. Just don't expect me to answer any spot quizzes, okay?'

She laughed, knowing arguing her relative normalcy was a pointless battle. Fake dates and colour-coded life plans didn't exactly paint a flattering picture. 'So what else did you learn?'

'Apart from about your fascinating teenage career as a newspaper delivery girl?' he said. 'Well, in addition to your dislike of red wine, you also don't like coriander.'

She grimaced. 'I really went all out with the mesmerising content, huh?'

Dan grinned. 'I wasn't bored,' he said, 'and I learnt all sorts of random stuff. Like that you went to school with my cousin—Melinda Halliday.'

Sophie nodded. 'Yes, I did. She was in the year above me at high school.'

She spoke without thinking, but immediately realised her mistake. She held her breath, waiting.

His brow wrinkled. 'I thought the file said you were twenty-nine?' he said. 'The same age as Mel?'

She breathed out slowly. Of *course* he was going to ask questions.

'I am,' she said, then paused, considering. How to explain? 'I…uh…had to skip a year.'

'Why?'

It was the obvious question, but the answer—not so much. There was a reason she'd left this little detail from her file, after much typing and deleting and typing and deleting.

Could she use Dan's line? *It's probably not first date conversation.*

She could, and it would have the added bonus of being the absolute truth. Stories of childhood illness didn't really set the scene for a hot and heavy first date, did they?

But this, of course, *wasn't* a real first date.

'Cancer,' she said simply. 'Mine. I was ten and in and out of hospital for months. I got so far behind at school I took the rest of the year off to recover and had to repeat.'

For a long moment Dan just stared at her, his face stiff with shock. When he spoke, his voice was rich with genuine concern. 'Oh, Soph, that's terrible.'

It was the first time he'd shortened her name. As if he was a friend, and not just part of her project plan.

'Uh-huh,' she said, with a weak attempt at a smile. 'That's one word for it.'

His expression quickly morphed from shock to concern. 'But are you okay now?'

She nodded. 'Yes, perfectly.'

The words slipped out effortlessly, as easily as if they'd been true. Oh, she'd beaten the cancer, but it hadn't left without a struggle—or without leaving its mark. At one time, in her teens, she'd imagined she'd done a deal with the devil: her life in exchange for her unborn children.

She was no longer that angsty, overly dramatic seventeen-year-old, but the reality remained. Chemotherapy had made her infertile. In an immovably permanent, no-chance-of-a-miracle-baby-*ever* kind of way.

'I don't normally tell people about it—being sick,' she said. 'I only tell people really close to me.'

'I'm sorry. I shouldn't have asked.'

She shook her head. 'Don't worry about it. I didn't have to tell you.'

It was true. She could have come up with something else. Her illness was an unlikely topic of conversation for the barbecue or the wedding, so a white lie wouldn't have done any harm to her project.

But she hadn't liked the idea of lying to him. For a relationship that had been formed solely to perpetuate a lie, it was an unexpected realisation.

Dan was just looking at her, his gaze exploring her face as if he was waiting for her to speak again. And she *should* speak, she knew. She kept almost doing it—almost opening her mouth to start saying the words where she'd tell him the *whole* truth.

Just so you know, I can't have children.

But she remained silent. Why?

Her decision always to announce to men her infertility like a newspaper headline—bold and harsh and up-front— meant she needed to get over this. This might not be a real date, and he had no prospect of becoming a real boyfriend, but why not practise with Dan?

Just so you know, I can't have children.

Just eight words. When she'd told him everything else. Why not this? She'd told total strangers that she was barren. Why not Dan?

He doesn't need to know.

A valid justification because—well, he *didn't*. Her ability or otherwise to carry a child was about as irrelevant and unrelated to their deal as it was possible to get.

But that wasn't the reason she wasn't telling him. She wasn't telling him because she didn't *want* him to know.

And she didn't want to even begin to analyse why that was.

It was a lovely meal, but Dan barely tasted a mouthful despite wiping his plate clean. It was Sophie rather than his tastebuds getting his full concentration.

She'd changed the subject, awkwardly and rapidly, from her illness to safer, more generic first date topics of conversation. Travel. Reality TV. Movies.

As she spoke he studied her. Not the upswept shimmer of her hair or the perfect paleness of her shoulders, nor the hint of cleavage the heart shaped neckline of her dress revealed—although he wasn't exactly ignoring any of those things. Instead, he studied her with fresh eyes.

His heart ached for the ten-year-old Sophie. He hated—*hated*—the idea of her being so sick and stuck for months in a hospital bed. Irrationally it made him angry—angry that it had happened to her and angry he hadn't been there to help her.

Although what good a sixteen-year-old boy who'd spent his every waking moment studying would have been to her he had no idea.

Maybe he could have held her hand.

'My birthday's October 20.'

She stilled, her fork and its piece of salmon hovering midway between her plate and mouth. 'Pardon me?'

'And I'm an only child.'

Her gaze sharpened, and then she smiled. 'The questionnaire?' she said.

'Yeah. Figured it couldn't hurt to answer a few of your questions.'

Especially when the past *she'd* just revealed left him humbled. Suddenly it seemed petty—juvenile, even—to hold his past so close to his chest. What she'd said in the café was true. He knew all about her, while she knew nothing about him.

'Thank you,' she said. 'Can I take notes?'

He laughed, even though he knew she was completely serious. Sophie didn't joke when it came to her project. 'I think you should quit while you're ahead.'

'Okay,' she conceded. 'Go on, then.'

She placed her fork on her plate and settled back in her chair, waiting.

'This feels like a job interview,' he said.

She took pity on him. 'Maybe we should combine what we both want. You want this to be like a normal date, and I want to tick an item off my project plan. So—' she reached forward, picking up her wine glass and taking a sip '—how about I pretend to be a particularly nosy first date…' he raised his eyebrows at that '…and you pretend to be the kind of guy who would *not* totally freak out if you were asked these questions on said first date.'

He nodded. 'Fine.'

'Good,' she said, then leant towards him, her voice low and unexpectedly sultry. 'So, Dan, what high school did you go to?'

He blinked at the incongruity of her tone and the question.

She grinned. 'I was trying to cancel out the job interview vibe.'

He leant closer himself, running his finger down her cheek before she had a chance to pull away. 'Goal achieved,' he said roughly.

'Oh, good,' she said, in a slightly uneven version of her project manager voice, straightening up in her chair. But her prim and proper act was far too late—heat radiated between them and warmed her cheeks to a deep pink.

He cleared his throat. 'Guildford Grammar,' he said.

'Ah, private school boy—I should have guessed,' she said with a teasing grin, and the tension eased—a little.

While they waited for dessert she peppered him with questions—where he went to university, how he liked his coffee, that sort of thing. Nothing too scary, even if he did feel the need to question the necessity of them every now and then. And Sophie always answered the same way: 'I like to be prepared.'

Finally she got to the question he'd been dreading.

'I think I already know the answer to this one,' she said with a smile across the two complicated looking desserts between them, 'but have you ever been married?'

He took a moment to respond, still questioning his decision to tell her the truth. He *never* spoke about his past. To anyone. As far as the women he dated were concerned he'd been allergic to commitment from birth.

Sophie filled the silence as she poked at her crème caramel with a spoon. 'I know—silly question. But I thought I should ask—'

'Yes, I have.'

The spoon clattered onto the fine china serving plate, smudging the chocolate sauce flourishes around the rim.

'What?' she said. 'I mean—sorry—uh—*when*?'

He counted back the years. It was a lifetime ago—a whole different version of Dan ago. 'I got married thirteen years ago. Divorced three years later.'

She still stared at him, agog. *'Wow.'* She tilted her head and chewed at her bottom lip. 'I thought maybe a woman was why you quit law, but I never thought you'd been the marrying type.'

'You thought a *woman* was why I bought my bar?' he asked, surprised she'd spent any time thinking about it at all. Maybe he shouldn't be—she probably considered it research for her project.

She nodded. 'Yeah, a few times you've gotten all tall, dark and distant—I put two and two together.'

'It wasn't a woman.' He paused. 'I just realised my life was on totally the wrong track.'

'The marrying-super-young track?' she asked. 'You must have only been—what?—twenty-two? Twenty-three?'

'Maybe,' he said. 'Although more likely the marrying-for-the-totally-wrong-reasons track.'

Her eyes widened with interest. 'And what were they?'

He met her gaze for a long moment. 'That wasn't on the questionnaire.'

Dan half expected her to push, but to his relief she just nodded with only slightly disappointed understanding.

'But can I ask just one more question?'

'How about we eat dessert and go back to pretending this is a normal date? Without the nosy question-asker?'

No such luck.

'It's an important one, and given I got the marriage one so wrong I really have to ask.' Her gaze flicked downwards, and she absently moved her spoon around her plate. 'Do you have any children?'

'No,' he said immediately. Too quickly, probably.

But Sophie didn't seem to notice. She laughed—maybe a little unnaturally—and said, 'I'm relieved I didn't read you completely wrong, then.' She scooped up a piece of dessert with her spoon, but didn't make a move to eat it. 'Would you do it again? I mean marriage?'

And repeat his past mistakes? Regress to the person he'd once been but now barely recognised?

'No,' he said. 'Never.'

CHAPTER SIX

The Sophie Project 2.1 (Project Manager: S. Morgan)
Note to self: Maintain professional distance from Dan
(Important!)

AFTER dinner they walked across the car park to a soundtrack of barely muffled music and loud conversation from the pub across the street. Sophie walked in silence beside him, glancing occasionally at the crowd almost spilling from the open ground-floor windows.

'Do you want to go in for a drink?' Dan asked.

'Oh, no,' she replied. 'I used to go there when I was at uni. We're not the target demographic. And besides, what I'm wearing is all wrong.'

He needed no excuse to run his gaze down the tailored lines of her dress. It was just like her, that dress—elegant, subtle, classic. And sexy. Very, very sexy.

'Who cares what you're wearing?'

The patrons he could see wore everything from collared shirts and sparkling tops through to dresses and shorts that had obviously come straight from the beach.

'I care,' she said. 'Besides, the agreement was dinner only. You don't have to do this.'

What if he wanted to? Not go to that pub, particularly, just spend more time with Sophie?

'Do you only ever do things you've planned?' he asked, coming to a stop in the middle of the car park, directly across from the entrance to the pub. 'Never try anything that isn't perfectly scheduled into one of your project plans?'

'Of course not,' she said. 'I can be spontaneous.'

'Great,' he said. 'Let's go grab a drink, then.'

He could see her battle with what to say. Argue—and prove his point—or acquiesce and walk into the pub—*shock! Horror!*—over dressed.

'Fine,' she said. 'One drink.'

'Watch out,' he said. 'Don't go all wild and crazy on me.'

She shot him a cutting look. 'I know how to have a good time.'

'Really?' he asked, remembering something she'd said that first night at his bar. 'Dinner parties and long walks on the beach with Rick, right?'

She went silent, staring down at her sparkling silver heels, and for a moment he was sure he'd gone too far. But then she surprised him by reaching out to grab his hand. Her eyes were bright. Determined.

With a tug, she pulled him towards the road. 'Come on,' she said. 'Let's go.'

She led him past the pair of burly bouncers and into the dimly lit and heaving pub. People were crammed into every inch of space in front of a window-framed backdrop of star-scattered sky and the thick black ocean beneath it.

Sophie had been right. He was easily ten years older than the majority of… No, make that *everyone* else there. Sophie's comparatively ancient status appeared to be doing her no harm, though—more than one young male head swivelled in her direction as she strode into the room. Make that a hell of a lot *more* than one young male head.

He used the hand she still held to slow her rapid pace

and to draw her closer towards him. Close enough that their shoulders bumped as they walked.

She shot him a questioning look but made no move to drop his hand. Good.

The crowd at the central bar was easily four deep, but Sophie guided them through to the front with absolutely no effort at all. At her destination, rather than ordering, she turned and leant against the polished chrome bar as if she owned the place.

'What can I get you?' she said. No. *Purred* was a more appropriate description.

Where was the woman who'd subconsciously plucked at the fabric of her dress when she'd answered the door—who had just two minutes ago anguished over the suitability of her clothing? He dropped her hand, searching her face for signs that this was all an act. For cracks in this sudden veneer of ultra-sophistication.

There were none.

A shove from amongst the crowd suddenly pushed him towards her, and for long, long seconds they were pressed together, chest to chest, hip to hip, thigh to thigh. Her softness against his hardness.

His hands had landed at her waist and she'd turned her face up to his, her eyes rapidly changing from shocked to... Well, he guessed he was looking at her in exactly the same way.

He swallowed a groan. They were as good as embracing already—it would be so easy to close the gap between their mouths and make it real.

Her tongue darted out, moistening her lips.

It was all the invitation he needed...

But as he shifted his weight forward, moments from the kiss he was beginning to think had always been inevitable, she sucked her full bottom lip between her teeth in a movement he'd seen her perform many times before. When think-ing. Worrying.

It was the crack in the veneer—an unwanted reminder that stopped him in his tracks.

He stepped back. 'I'll have a bourbon,' he said.

She closed her eyes, her black mascaraed lashes a harsh contrast to her porcelain skin.

When she opened them again Miss Sophistication was back, and she smiled brightly, not meeting his gaze, before turning to order their drinks.

Minutes later, drinks in hand, they managed to fight their way through the masses to a coveted space near a window. The evening ocean breeze tugged long strands of Sophie's hair free of whatever women called the complicated roll she'd fashioned her blond mane into.

She took a long drink of her cocktail, meeting his gaze over the rim. 'I'm not as boring as you think I am.'

'I never said you were boring.'

'Lacking spontaneity, then,' she said.

He shrugged. 'That's kind of unavoidable when you live your life to an immovable, predetermined schedule.'

'I don't,' she said. 'I know how strange my project plan is. But it's a one-off thing—a guide to getting my life back on track.'

'But it isn't the project plan that had you stressing about where we were going tonight, and umming and ahhing out in the car park before.'

'I came for a drink, didn't I?' she said, nodding at the mar-tini glass in her hand. 'And, for your information, I *did* have fun when I lived in Sydney. Rick preferred to stay at home, but I'd go out with my girlfriends, or hit King Street Wharf on a Friday after work.'

Now he could add *dull* to Rick's list of sins.

'But you *did* plan that fun, didn't you? Organise it a few

days in advance? Take clothes to change into after work? That sort of thing?'

Sophie opened her mouth to disagree, than snapped it shut before nodding with much reluctance.

'So you might not have had a project plan stuck on your fridge, but it was there nonetheless.'

She narrowed her eyes, shifting from *deny* to *defend*. 'Fine. If, like you say, I *am* marginally over-organised, what's wrong with that? Why is it wrong to want some control over my life?'

'Is that what it is?' he asked. 'You need to be in control?'

She slowly shook her head. 'No, that's the wrong word. It's, uh…' Her forehead creased in concentration. 'I guess I like how when I put something on a list it happens. And then you cross it off and it's gone.' A shadow passed across her face. 'Even the bad stuff.'

He stepped towards her automatically—to do what, he didn't know. Touch her arm? Hold her?

He forced himself to do neither. Accidental top-to-toe contact might have been okay at the bar, but touching her now would certainly cross whatever line they were both dancing so close to.

'What bad stuff?' he asked.

For what felt like minutes she stared at him, deep into his eyes. Assessing him. Chewing her bottom lip again.

She placed her glass down gently on the windowsill. 'When I was sick, my mum had a calendar of all of my treatments. On the fridge, actually. We'd talk about what was going to happen, and how it was going to make me better—so even though it was scary I always knew what was going on.' She paused as the crowd around them cheered the opening bars of an iconic Australian rock anthem, then raised her voice to be heard over the resultant joyful, drunken singalong. 'And then we'd come home from the hospital and I'd put a big red cross over that treatment because it was done. Gone.'

She shrugged. She had spoken in the matter-of-fact tone of someone who had figured something out long ago.

But had she really?

He realised that the woman who'd dragged him into the bar was the same woman he'd seen glimpses of before—a sparkle in her gaze here, a teasing comment there. It was as if she was wearing her super-organisation like armour, only occasionally letting people see the real Sophie through the chinks.

He wanted to see more of that Sophie.

But how to encourage her to take detours off the path she'd mapped out for herself?

He might not have had a project plan, but he knew all about travelling full steam ahead with blinkers on down the wrong path. Not that his solution—quitting his job, buying a pub and swearing off serious relationships—would be of much use to her.

Sophie was watching him, waiting for him to say something. Her brows were drawn together as she over-thought whatever she imagined he was about to say, making him want to reach out and rub those worried lines away.

Beside her a couple barely out of their teens began to kiss enthusiastically, and then a board-shorts-wearing man with bleached blond hair came within millimetres of sloshing beer down Sophie's dress as he barrelled obliviously past.

They couldn't have this conversation here. They shouldn't even *be* here. His interest in walking in had been driven purely by Sophie's reluctance to do so.

'This place is awful,' he said. 'Do you want to go?'

Sophie nodded eagerly. 'I'm sure I've reached my spontaneity quota for the night.'

A few minutes later they were outside, and the breeze had

cooled enough for Sophie to hug her arms as she walked. He had no jacket to offer her, so he did what felt natural—he wrapped his arm around her shoulders, pulling her close.

At his touch she paused mid-stride, turned to look at him. Her height and her heels raised her to near his eye-level, resulting in a negligible gap between her lips and his. Convenient.

'Very chivalrous—but a little touchy-feely for a first date, don't you think?' she said, but made absolutely no effort to move away.

He responded by tugging her closer, turning slightly towards her to block suddenly stronger gusts of wind. 'No,' he said. 'Do you?'

She was shaking her head almost before he'd asked the question. 'I guess not.'

They started walking again, the distance to his car annoyingly short. He liked how she fitted against him—how they almost instantly figured out a perfect rhythm to their walk.

Part of him questioned what the *hell* he was doing. Touching her. Considering the practicalities of kissing her. Wondering if maybe it wouldn't be *that* bad an idea to make this date one hundred percent real.

But it was only a small part of him doing the questioning. The vast majority—capitulating pathetically to the will of his baser self—thought that wrapping his arm around her was the best idea ever and had all sorts of plans. Starting with taking advantage of how little distance there was between their mouths.

They reached the car, and rather than unlocking the doors he found himself turning Sophie so her hips and lower back brushed against the passenger side window.

More strands of her hair had pulled loose and whipped about in the breeze. A dull cheer originated from the pub as yet another mid-eighties classic blasted out onto the street.

He'd dropped his arm from her shoulders, and while he still stood close they didn't touch at all.

Sophie was thinking. He could as good as see the pros and cons list he was sure she was rapidly constructing in her mind, and knew he should probably be doing the same.

Kissing Sophie:
Pro: I get to kiss Sophie.
Con: …

Ah. No prizes for guessing which part of him was writing that list.

'You think it's stupid, don't you—all my planning and crossing off of things?'

'No,' he said, imagining a tiny version of Sophie standing in the same kitchen he'd been in earlier that night, a red pen gripped tightly in her hand. 'Not stupid. Brave.'

'Maybe when I was ten.'

'No,' he said. 'Not just then.'

'I needed something after what happened with Rick—to focus on, you know?' She dropped her chin, focusing on the small stitched logo on the left side of his chest. 'But I guess I sometimes take it a little too far.' She laughed—a hollow sound. 'And start to verge into obsessive/crazy territory.'

He reached out, tucking a finger beneath her chin and dragging her gaze back to his. 'You aren't crazy. And I can relate to being a little obsessive about a goal.'

'With your bar, do you mean?'

He nodded. 'Yeah.'

And his previous career. And university. And his marriage.

She shook her head, and his hand fell away from her face. 'You're nothing like me. You *are* spontaneous. You have fun with women, you totally change your career and can even agree to be a total stranger's fake wedding date.' She sighed noisily. 'Geez, if some guy had asked *me* to do something like this I probably would have whipped out a damn SWOT analysis.'

'A what?'

'Strengths, weaknesses, opportunities, threats…' Another long sigh. 'My God. I *am* boring, aren't I?'

He smiled. 'Wrong again.'

'You're just being nice.'

He leant forward, close enough so his shirt just brushed against her chest and he could whisper into her ear. 'You know what, Soph? I'm really not that nice a guy.'

To prove his point, his hands stole out, sliding up to rest at her waist. Not lightly. *Firm.*

'I've had an idea about how you can shake things up. A small diversion from your project plan.'

Despite all that she'd just said, she stiffened. 'I can't drop anything from the plan. I *do* need to find a job, and go to the wedding, and—'

He ran his thumbs gently up and down her sides in an attempt to distract the cogs working overtime in her brain. 'Don't panic—the plan stays. I just think it will do you good to have a little fun along the way. Be more spontaneous.'

'And does this fun by any chance involve you?'

His breath was hot against the delicate skin beneath her ear. 'If you're interested.'

Okay, so it wasn't an entirely selfless suggestion.

She pulled back just a little—enough to give her room to twist slightly in his arms and meet his gaze. A streetlamp illuminated her satiny skin and reflected off her cobalt-blue eyes.

'What exactly are you suggesting?'

'Doing what I'm pretty sure we both want to do.'

It was too dim to see the blush that flushed her cheeks, but he knew it was there.

'I thought you said that you and I would never work.'

'I've changed my mind,' he said. And he had. He'd been so sure that starting anything with Sophie could only end badly—that he'd only add to the hurt she was already experiencing. But maybe he'd had it all wrong. As long as they both knew the score, why *not* explore this unarguable attraction between them? Maybe a distraction—an activity that was certainly *not* on her project plan—was exactly what she needed?

'But you don't do relationships.'

Now it was his turn to go tense in her arms. Here it was— proof positive as to why this was terrible, horrible—the *worst* idea. He was thinking of a hot kiss up against the car and how badly he wanted to see Sophie in the new underwear she was going to buy—and then remove it as quickly as possible— while she jumped straight to talking about *relationships*.

'I don't,' he said, the words triggering the slightest tightening of Sophie's jaw. 'But I do flings. Why don't we have one? A no-strings-attached, *spontaneous* fling from now until the wedding? With the added bonus of avoiding the need to lie to your friends. At the wedding we would really be together.'

'But not in a relationship?'

'No.'

The corner of her mouth kicked up, but there was no sparkle in her eyes. 'And this is going to be *good* for me? Is this your version of helping me out—a bit of charity for the sad, recently dumped and compulsive maker of lists?' She pressed her palms to his chest and gave a light shove. 'Thanks, but no thanks.'

He stepped back, but let his hands fall from her slowly. Reluctantly. He shrugged. 'Sophie, I like you. I *want* you. And I think we could have fun together. Charitable is the last thing I'm feeling right now.'

Instead he was itching with the need to touch her again, to

drag her into his arms and kiss her the way he badly wanted to. To convince her with his body after totally failing with his words.

He made himself take a further step away from her, and reached into his pocket for his keys. Sophie had leant back against the car, her head turned as she gazed out across the deserted beach and beyond to the inky black sea.

With a press on his key the car was unlocked, and Dan strode around the car to the driver's side door. Sophie pushed away from the window and turned to open her door just as he opened his. Across the patent black roof of the car their eyes met.

'If you change your mind, Soph, all you have to do is say the word.'

CHAPTER SEVEN

The Sophie Project 2.1 (Project Manager: S. Morgan)
New Task: Visit to Fremantle (not a date)

WHEN Sophie pulled into the wine bar's car park fifteen minutes prior to the start of her Saturday night shift Dan was leaning against the hood of his car, watching her.

Waiting for her?

She pretended not to notice as she climbed out of the car and swung her handbag over her shoulder. Ignoring him was hard work—because it would be so much easier to let the heat of his undivided attention incinerate all the sensible, logical, *necessary* decisions she'd made.

Like not agreeing to a no-strings-attached fling with Dan.

That was the big one. But that decision was the culmination of a whole heap of smaller but equally important ones. Because as they'd stood beside his car after their date, her skin goosepimpling and her body shivering for reasons unrelated to the buffeting breeze, she'd had many tough choices to make.

For example, when his hand had curled around her waist she could have a) Brushed him off. Stepped aside. Something! Or b) Done nothing.

And then, later, when he'd made the boundaries of his suggestion crystal clear—that anything between them could only ever be temporary—she'd warred with herself. *Could* she shove aside her logical self and seize the moment? *Could* she, a woman who had only a series of committed relationships behind her, really let go and leap into the madness that would be a fling with Dan?

She'd been so close—*so* close—to answering yes. But then her logical self had piped up, loud and obnoxious: *He feels sorry for you. He thinks ruffling the feathers of crazy project plan lady would practically be a community service. And, even worse: You like him. He'll hurt you.*

That realisation had made her last decision easy.

Slide her hands up his chest to: a) Creep higher to loop behind his neck and pull him closer. Or b) Push him away.

And so she had—although it hadn't felt as right as she'd hoped. That little throwaway comment across the roof of the car hadn't helped either, but she'd managed to restrain herself from doing or saying something unwise throughout the whole drive home. Dan's apparent ability to instantly forget that he'd just propositioned her had made that a heck of a lot easier too. He'd been clearly far from cut up over her rejection.

Humph.

So now she walked across the car park, all senses in overdrive as her brain over-analysed the situation and her body over-reacted to the force of his gaze. Avoiding him was impossible as he'd parked right beside the rear entrance to the wine bar. And there wasn't even a reason *to* avoid him— apart from the certain knowledge that the amount of time she spent with Dan was inversely proportional to the strength of her self control. Not that she thought she'd jump him in the middle of a public car park, of course…

'Right on time,' he said as she slowed to a stop in front of him. He didn't move from his position propped against the car, his legs crossed at the ankles.

She nodded. 'I always am.'

He grinned, reaching with a strong tanned hand to slide his sunglasses off. He wasn't in any of the uniforms she was familiar with—not the beach uniform or the bartender one. Instead he wore jeans and a slim-fitting charcoal T-shirt that clung to the width of his biceps.

'Always?' he said, raising his eyebrows. 'You never lose track of time? Sleep in? Get distracted?'

'No. That's what alarm clocks are for.'

He looked a little stunned. 'So you've never been late for work—ever?'

She laughed. 'Of course I have. Ferry strikes, that sort of thing.'

'But only when it was outside of your control?'

She nodded, again. 'Yes.'

'Never taken a sick day when you weren't sick? Never wagged a day off school, right?'

'Of course not!' she said. 'I would *never* do that.'

Again that cheeky grin. 'Calm down. I'm not impugning your character, here. Just setting the scene.'

She eyed him warily. 'For what, exactly?'

He pushed away from the car and opened the passenger side door with a flourish. 'Climb in,' he said. 'We're blowing off work today.'

It took her a moment to grasp what he was saying. 'Pardon me?'

'We're taking the night off. I thought we could go into Fremantle. Watch the sunset or something. I could show you the other bar.'

'Take the night off?'

'Uh-huh. It's a pretty simple concept.'

She shook her head. 'Why would we do that?'

'Because we can. I'm the boss, and choosing when I take time off is a big perk.' He shrugged. 'It's really not that big a deal. Come on—it'll be fun.'

'But the whole reason I'm working here is because you're understaffed. This doesn't make any sense.'

Finally Dan seemed to realise that she wasn't going to obediently leap into his car, and he swung the door shut with a heavy, muffled, this-is-an-expensive-car-sounding thud. A bit different from the creaking slam that was all her mum's little red hatchback could manage.

'That was last week. I've hired a new bartender and one of my waitresses is back from sick leave. The bar will survive without us for one night.'

'Does that mean the bar doesn't need me at all any more?'

'No, just not tonight.'

'Hmm.' She looked at him sceptically. 'Look, maybe we should go back to my original plan to pay you to be my wedding date. You don't need an extraneous, only mildly competent waitress. Our deal has to be fair.'

Plus, if she paid him, it pushed the agreement back into pure-business-deal territory. After last night they certainly needed a good shove back onto the straight and narrow. She really didn't want Dan having any ideas that she might change her mind.

And *she* definitely didn't want to be having those kinds of ideas, either...

'The deal stands,' he said, his tone firm. 'University exams start in a week, and some of my staff are taking time off. I still need you—just not tonight.'

'Then why didn't you just call to cancel my shift?'

She knew she was being difficult, but she was stalling. *Was* he just planning to pick things up from where they'd left off last night?

Dan took a long, deep breath. 'Because this isn't in the plan. We're low on reservations so I decided to take the night off and go have some fun. With you. That's it. And I didn't call because you never would have agreed over the phone.'

True. Distance from Dan always had a positive impact on her ability to think straight.

'I'm not going to change my mind,' she said, unable to look at him as she spoke. There was no need to clarify what she meant.

'I know.'

Her eyes flicked back up to his. If she ignored the charged atmosphere between them—and she had to, because her only other option was to abandon the project and put as much space between herself and Dan as possible—she could tell herself this wasn't about their fling. Or rather, the fling they weren't going to have. So why? Why take her to Fremantle? He'd already made it clear he didn't want a relationship, so he couldn't be asking her out on a real date.

'Oh, is this to replace the fake date we've got planned for next week? Doesn't Wednesday work for you any more?'

Yes, remember: *it's all about the project.*

She started mentally shifting her plan around. Moving next week's task up a few days wouldn't hurt. In fact, it…

Dan took a step forward, and now they were centimetres apart. His nearness scrambled her thoughts and heated her skin.

'This has nothing to do with your project,' he said. Low and quiet. 'Let's go to Fremantle for absolutely no reason at all. Not because of your project, but just because we can.'

He gaze locked on hers—and then, for the first time in as long as she remembered, she ignored all the sensible, sane lists of reasons in her head and did something totally unexpected. And definitely unwise.

Sophie nodded. 'Okay,' she said. 'Let's go.'

Rather than climbing into Dan's car, Sophie had made him follow her home—both to return her mother's car and so she could change.

He really shouldn't have been surprised.

But then, when she'd walked down the driveway in a floaty green dress that nipped in at her waist and showed off her fabulous legs, well, any niggling frustration at her obsession with appropriate clothing was swiftly forgotten. That dress was well worth waiting a few minutes for.

And those legs…

He was doubly pleased that she'd agreed to come out with him. Although for a while there it had seemed far from certain. In the car park she'd studied him with calculating eyes, weighing up every word he'd spoken as she searched and searched for the *why*.

But the thing was, there wasn't one. Not really. It was as simple as realising that it was going to be an unusually quiet night at the bar and suddenly having the—*he*'d thought— brilliant idea of spending the evening in Fremantle instead. With Sophie.

He hadn't bothered figuring out *why*. He'd just decided that was what he wanted to do. And he had the vague sense that it wouldn't do Sophie any harm to do something so out of the blue. It was becoming a habit, this compulsion to push her a little off-balance—to see that fire in her eyes as she threw everything into sticking to her plan.

They drove to Fremantle engaged in easy conversation, avoiding their wedding date agreement entirely. They discussed Sophie's job hunting so far—good, with a few interviews lined up the following week—and his opinion on the best beaches in Perth—Cottesloe and Scarborough. By the time they drove into the port city Sophie was smiling at him like a woman living in the moment—one without spreadsheets and to-do lists and project plans.

They parked in the centre of town, detouring through the century-old Fremantle Markets on their way to the beach. They walked past stall after stall of fresh fruit and vegetables before entering 'the hall'—a maze of handicrafts and souvenirs and food and—well—everything else you could think of. It was packed with locals and tourists, and the scent of incense battled with spices, fragrant candles and buttered popcorn. Here they took their time—Sophie looking at handmade jewellery, Dan buying a paper cone filled with candy-covered hazelnuts.

He paused outside a shop he hadn't been to in years. So long ago he'd forgotten it had even existed.

'Oh, how cool!' Sophie said, stepping past him and walking inside. He followed her to the far wall, where she perused such fine wares as rubber vomit, whoopee cushions and fake dog poop.

'My dad used to bring me here when I was a kid,' he said. 'As a reward for getting good grades, I could choose whatever I wanted.'

Picking up a bag of hot chilli lollies, Sophie grinned at him. 'Your mum must have loved that.'

'She was a pretty good sport, really. Although the fake cockroaches in her bed didn't go down quite as well as I'd expected.'

Sophie laughed. 'I can imagine.'

She put the lollies back and then examined the intriguingly labelled 'Pot of Snot'. 'So you did well at school?' she asked.

'With fake mucus on offer? Of course.'

She nodded. 'Yeah, me too—just without the bodily fluids. I was kind of obsessed with studying.'

He slapped a hand to his chest in mock surprise. 'No!'

She raised an eyebrow. 'Very funny,' she said dryly.

'I was the same,' he said. 'Nose in a textbook every night and all weekend.'

She turned to face him, rubber chicken in hand. 'You are the *last* guy I would have guessed to be such a good student. I would have picked you to be the guy making out with the most popular girl at school behind the sports shed—not the one studying away in the library.'

He met her eyes. 'Who says I didn't do both?'

She blushed, swinging the forgotten chicken absently from its feet. 'I should have known.'

The chicken smacked against the side of the display table, squeaking in distress. This earned them both a stern look from the shopkeeper, so they made a hasty retreat, grinning at each other. Back in the crammed maze of aisles, they followed the swell of bodies out onto South Terrace. Lined with cafés and restaurants, the busiest street in Fremantle was packed with everyone from retirees to families to the terribly trendy. Plus, of course, the definitive bohemian Fremantle residents—musicians and artists adorned with dreadlocks, piercings and colourful clothing.

'Where to now?' Sophie asked, holding up a hand to shield against the glare of the rapidly setting sun.

'The beach, I think—for the sunset.'

'We'll miss it,' she said. 'We're too late.'

Dan shook his head. 'Too far to *walk*, maybe. Follow me.'

He braced himself for a barrage of questions, but they never came. Instead she let him lead her down a side street, and he began to hope that this was all going to be *way* easier than he'd imagined. Until she saw where they were headed.

'No way,' she said, and stopped dead on the foot path. Ahead sat a neat row of scooters behind a red-and-white 'For Hire' sign. 'I don't do motorbikes.'

'They aren't exactly motorbikes.'

'Close enough,' she said, crossing her arms. 'They're dangerous.'

'Not if we keep to the back streets and go slow. It'll be fine.'

She shook her head firmly. 'No. Look, I know tonight is all about me being spontaneous and everything—but there is no way I'm getting on one of those things. They freak me out. One little nudge and it's all over.'

'It's safe, Sophie—really. Not that you need one for these things, but I've got a motorcycle licence. I'll look after you.'

'You and your licence are welcome to go for a spin. I'll just wait here.'

Dan shoved his hands roughly into his pockets. 'Would it help if I went and asked the owner about his safety record? Surely statistical analysis would reassure you?'

'Nice try, but no. I have no interest in wavering from my four-wheel motorised vehicle policy.'

He'd known Sophie would resist his brainwave of hiring scooters, but this was getting ridiculous.

'Fine,' he said. 'We don't have time to go back to the car, so how about we get a ta—?'

'Oh, look!' she exclaimed, walking to the end of the second row of scooters. 'Why don't we hire *this*?'

She pointed at a two-person, four-wheeled—importantly—golf buggy/scooter amalgamation. Painted on its side, in childish lettering was its name: '*Scoot Car.*'

'No,' he said. It was tiny, bright yellow and had more than a passing resemblance to a circus vehicle. The type usually overflowing with men wearing wigs and with white-painted faces. *He* would look like a clown if he folded his six-foot-one body inside it.

'But it's safer than a scooter. It's perfect!'

'There is no way I'm getting in that thing, Sophie.'

Understanding seemed to dawn, and she grinned a wicked grin. 'What, Dan? Are *you* worried about looking silly? The man who told me just last night that I shouldn't care what other people think?'

She had him, he knew. 'We're barely going to fit. We're both going to look silly.'

She shrugged, her eyes sparkling. 'I don't care, Dan. I'm being *spontaneous*!'

With a sigh, he went and paid the hire fee.

A few minutes later they were settled in the buggy, Sophie nervously fiddling with the hem of her skirt, running her fingers along the swirls of decorative stitching.

Sensing his eyes on her, she stilled her hands. 'Don't crash,' she said, with a pointed look.

'You just told me how safe this is,' he said. It earned him a glare. He winked at her. 'I'll do my best.'

They scooted slowly—because the buggy had a top speed of forty kilometres an hour and *not* because of Sophie's death grip on the handrail—through the criss-cross streets of Georgian and Edwardian cottages.

Slowly the whiteness eased out of her knuckles and Sophie relaxed back into her seat. 'This is nice,' she said as they left the town centre and headed towards the beach, the salty sea breeze caressing their skin.

He agreed. The close confines of the buggy pressed Sophie's thigh against his, leaving only a thin layer of cotton and denim between them. Their shoulders collided with every bump and crack in the road, and their feet fought for space in the narrow footwell.

It should have felt cramped and uncomfortable, but it didn't. Instead he struggled to concentrate on the road rather than the woman beside him. And to control the buggy rather than his body's reaction to her.

It didn't take long to get to the beach, and he pulled off the road at a hill that offered uninterrupted views of the rapidly setting sun where it looked to be hovering mere centimetres above the infinite horizon.

'Just in time,' Sophie said, making no move to climb out of the buggy. Neither did he.

They sat in silence as the sun made its lazy dive into the

ocean. Long, long minutes while their bodies touched and they both stared straight ahead, as if in denial of the fizz and hiss of the sparks flying between them.

He wasn't about to lie to himself—of *course* he wanted Sophie to change her mind. But he wasn't crass enough to have planned tonight purely for that purpose—he did, genuinely, just want to spend time with her. Which was odd in itself.

In the past ten years he'd taken women to restaurants, cocktail bars, concerts, shows…hotel rooms. But never on an unplanned, rambling exploration of Fremantle. Or anything even resembling what they were doing.

Except, of course, this *wasn't* a date.

It was difficult to believe that when the urge to turn and kiss her was near-overwhelming.

But he couldn't. Not yet. She had to say the word. As badly as he wanted Sophie, he couldn't kiss her unless she knew exactly what she was signing up for. A fling. Short-term.

It was all he was capable of.

The tension was almost a physical thing—thick and heavy. Sophie could have cut it with a knife if it had been in any way possible to squeeze one between them.

Which it wasn't. She was terribly—and wonderfully— aware of exactly how they were sandwiched together.

There had been a moment when the little, buzzing scooter- buggy had rolled to a stop and she could have stepped out. Created that tension-defusing space they so badly needed.

Ever since she'd agreed to join him tonight the tension had been growing. And growing. She'd told herself it was all just fun and easy and meaningless. *Ha!* A wasted effort.

But acknowledging that she liked him and wanted nothing more than to turn *right this instant* and touch her lips to his achieved nothing. Because she knew she couldn't handle a fling with Dan Halliday.

She just had to accept it—she was a serious relationship kind of girl. Keeping things platonic was the sensible, *right* thing to do. Even if they'd well overstepped 'businesslike', there was no reason they couldn't complete the rest of the project as, well, friends.

But they were never going to achieve that if they continued to sit in silence, doing nothing to shatter the tension cocooning them and escalating with every second.

She cleared her throat, the sound awkward above the distant splash of waves and the squawking chatter of seagulls.

'It's weird how we were so similar as teenagers and are so totally different now,' she said, trying her best to sound calm and relaxed and *not* as if she was pressed thigh to thigh to the most attractive man she'd ever met. 'I still can't get my head around it.'

'You kissed the most popular girl in school, too?' he said, shooting her a teasing grin.

She shoved against him lightly with her shoulder—not that she had to move far. 'You know what I mean. Head in a book, totally focussed on studying. It just doesn't seem to *fit* you, you know?'

He shrugged. 'Maybe it never did.'

They both stared straight ahead, their gazes not wavering from the sliver of a semi-circle that was all that remained of the sun.

'Do you mean you didn't *want* to study so hard? Did your parents put a lot of pressure on you?'

She'd been lucky—in a way. The pressure she'd put on herself had been completely self imposed. She'd hated being put down a year and had been determined to prove that it wasn't because she was stupid—as some heartless kids had teased. It hadn't taken long for success—and the need to achieve it—to become a habit.

'No,' he said, and then after a long pause added, 'Maybe a

little. But don't get me wrong—I wasn't one of those unfortunate kids forced to follow their parents' dreams. I wanted to be a lawyer as much as they wanted it. Actually more, I think. I associated law with success and recognition—and a lot of sillier things that are important to a seventeen-year-old like fancy cars and a beautiful wife.'

Wife, he'd said. Not girlfriend.

'Is that what you meant when you said you had experience in obsessing over goals? Was that to do with your career?' Then she added, before she lost her nerve, 'Your marriage?'

His gaze swung back out to sea just as the sun finally sank beneath its blue-black surface.

He swallowed, and the hands that had been resting relaxed on his lap tightened into fists.

'I'm sorry,' she said. 'It's none of my—'

'Yes,' he said.

But that was it. He made no move to elaborate further.

Questions waited impatiently on the tip of her tongue, but she didn't say a word, knowing that pushing Dan was a sure-fire way to end this conversation. And she wanted him to keep on talking. Not just because she couldn't fully comprehend his spectacular metamorphosis from what he'd once been to the languorous, live-in-the-moment player he now was. But because she wanted to understand him.

Finally, after even the last dawdling rays of sunset had seeped out of the sky, he spoke.

'I won't do it again. Get so caught up in where I'm going that I completely lose touch with what's happening in the moment.'

'What *was* happening?'

He shook his head. 'It doesn't matter.'

But obviously it did. It was evident in every rigid line of his body.

She wanted to ask him more, but there was no point. He'd

as good as constructed a wall between them—liberally plastered with 'Keep Out' signs.

'Is that what you think *I'm* doing?' she asked instead.

'Missing out on what's happening in the moment?' He turned towards her, his eyes locking with hers and seeing right into her soul. 'Missing out on what could happen *right now*?'

No. They couldn't. *She* couldn't.

It would be easier if she could drag her gaze away from his, but it was an impossible task. His lazy exploration of her face…her lips…it was hypnotising.

She closed her eyes. 'What would be the point?'

'Of doing something not on your project plan?'

She bristled, snapping out of her almost-stupor. 'Don't be ridiculous. Whatever you might think, I don't live every aspect of my life to some pre-packaged schedule.'

He didn't say a word, but his expression was blatantly disbelieving.

No longer were the cramped confines of the buggy a good thing. Despite its open sides, the vehicle was suddenly absurdly suffocating.

Sophie launched herself out of her seat, stumbling on the bitumen in her haste for distance. She strode away—one stride, two, three…

Where was she going?

She came to a halt, her arms crossed, staring at absolutely nothing.

She wasn't the type of person to flounce away from an argument.

Maybe she would be if she made it a task in her project plan…

No! Dan was *wrong*.

'Sophie?'

She jumped, surprised to hear Dan's voice directly behind

her. She didn't move even when his fingers curled gently around her upper arm.

'I get why you have your lists and plans, Soph,' he said, standing close enough that she could feel his body heat. 'But you're not a little girl any more. Maybe it's time to relax a little—let life happen rather than planning it all.'

She shrugged away from his touch, spinning around to face him. 'What's so wrong with having a plan, really, Dan? It's worked out well for me so far—school, career, *everything*.'

'Everything? How about Rick?'

She went totally still, stunned. 'I don't project manage my love life,' she said coolly. 'I didn't exactly require a written selection criteria.'

'Except now?'

'This isn't real.' She sighed heavily in frustration. 'I know this isn't normal. I *told* you it wasn't normal.' She paused, meeting his eyes in what remained of the fading light. 'And what do you suggest I do instead, exactly? Be more like you, perhaps?' She paused. 'And who exactly would *that* be?'

'Not more like me, Sophie. More like *you*.'

The strange words tumbled about in her head for long, long seconds.

'I *am* me.'

'Are you? That life you had in Sydney with Rick—was that what you really *wanted*, or what you'd always *planned*?'

These words she couldn't process. Not right now. She'd been happy in Sydney with Rick. It had been what she'd always wanted. Hadn't it?

'Why do you care, Dan?'

'Because, like I said, I know what can happen.'

'So, what? You feel the urge to share your cautionary tale with every person you meet?'

'No,' he said. 'Just you.'

Get FREE BOOKS and a FREE GIFT when you play the...

LAS VEGAS
GAME

Just scratch off the gold box with a coin. Then check below to see the gifts you get!

YES! I have scratched off the gold box.
Please send me my **2 FREE BOOKS** and **gift for which I qualify.** I understand that I am under no obligation to purchase any books as explained on the back of this card.

DETACH AND MAIL CARD TODAY! ▼

☐ I prefer the regular-print edition
116/316 HDL FNMS

☐ I prefer the larger-print edition
186/386 HDL FNMS

FIRST NAME

LAST NAME

ADDRESS

APT.#

CITY

STATE / PROV.

ZIP / POSTAL CODE

Worth TWO FREE BOOKS plus a BONUS Mystery Gift!

Worth TWO FREE BOOKS!

TRY AGAIN!

Offer limited to one per household and not applicable to series that subscriber is currently receiving. All orders subject to credit approval. Please allow 4 to 6 weeks for delivery.

Your Privacy—The Reader Service is committed to protecting your privacy. Our Privacy Policy is available online at www.ReaderService.com or upon request from the Reader Service. We make a portion of our mailing list available to reputable third parties that offer products we believe may interest you. If you prefer that we not exchange your name with third parties, or if you wish to clarify or modify your communication preferences, please visit us at www.ReaderService.com/consumerschoice or write to us at Reader Service Preference Service, P.O. Box 9062, Buffalo, NY 14269. Include your complete name and address.

© 2011 HARLEQUIN ENTERPRISES LIMITED. Printed in the U.S.A. ® and ™ are trademarks owned and used by the trademark owner and/or its licensee.

The Reader Service — Here's how it works:

BUSINESS REPLY MAIL
FIRST-CLASS MAIL   PERMIT NO. 717   BUFFALO, NY

POSTAGE WILL BE PAID BY ADDRESSEE

THE READER SERVICE
PO BOX 1867
BUFFALO NY 14240-9952

NO POSTAGE
NECESSARY
IF MAILED
IN THE
UNITED STATES

It derailed her momentarily.

'Why me?' He looked a little off-balance, as if unsure of the reason himself. 'Why do you want to fix *me*?'

'I don't want to fix you.'

'You just think I'm living my life all wrong.' She gave a short little humourless laugh. 'That's all.' And it hurt. A lot. It was just what she needed—someone else who didn't think she was good enough.

'No, I don't. I like you, Sophie.'

He said it as if that explained everything.

'Why are you so upset?' he continued, as the streetlights flickered on behind them, providing enough light to outline the sharp line of his jaw. 'Why care what I think if I have it so wrong?'

She shook her head. 'You *are* wrong. I'm not the automaton you think I am.' She stepped towards him, driven by a bottomless ache inside her. 'I think and react…' She pressed one palm to his chest, and pushed once—hard. But he didn't move. Not even a centimetre. 'And *feel*…'

All the fight faded from her against the immovable wall of Dan. She dipped her head, the hand on his chest curling as it relaxed and just lay there defeated for a moment.

But before it could fall away, and before she could succumb to the prickle of unwanted tears, his hand covered hers, holding it where it lay.

His other hand tipped her chin up.

'I know you feel, Soph.'

When you let yourself.

Maybe he wasn't thinking those words, but Sophie was. She as good as heard them—crystal clear and unforgiving.

And *right*.

Who was she kidding? It had taken her *six months* to let out all the pain that Rick had inflicted—and even that had been to a total stranger in a bar. Six months of distracting herself, keeping her mind busy—planning her holiday and planning her new life.

She'd been staring determinedly at a tiny freckle on Dan's cheek, but now she let her gaze wander to his eyes.

How did she feel about Dan? Attracted to him, definitely. And she liked him, too. Enough to know that what she was about to do was a very stupid idea.

But that was exactly why she was going to do it.

One kiss—how could it hurt, really? Could it hurt to succumb to the tingles that rocketed through her body whenever he touched her? To the urge to make his heart, beating so strongly beneath her palm, thump even faster—for her?

She left her right hand where it lay, let her left hand creep up and behind his neck, her fingers brushing against his short-cropped hair. She stood on her tiptoes, her attention flickering between his eyes and his mouth.

Ah, there it goes, she thought, as the pitter-patter of his heart accelerated nicely.

'Are you sure, Soph? I thought you didn't want this?'

She raised an eyebrow, her lips a whisper from his. 'Really, Dan. I'm trying to be spontaneous and you're going to analyse it? I'm living in the moment—just like you said.'

She'd meant to kiss him then—to lean that little bit closer and cover his mouth with hers.

But he beat her to it. *He* kissed *her*.

His mouth was firm. Warm. Nice.

No, nice was completely the wrong word. *Amazing. Perfect. Right.*

His arm wrapped around her, pulling her close. His heart raced, and so did hers. Her body shivered at the sweep of his hand across her back—hot through the thin cotton of her dress.

His tongue brushed against her bottom lip and she instantly deepened the kiss, exploring the shape of lips, his teeth, his tongue.

The hand on his heart slid upwards, a casualty of her almost desperate need to feel his heat. Her hand threaded into his hair and would have pulled him closer if doing so had been physically possible.

The kiss went on and on, their mouths breaking apart only to reunite at different angles. Her hands roamed over his shoulders, his over her back, her waist.

Sophie's head and body spun with sensation and the electricity of her body's reaction. She could feel *his* body's reaction against her belly. A warning that she really needed to take a step backwards. And soon—before this went too far.

Just not yet.

In the end it was Dan who broke the kiss, dragging his lips away from hers and breathing in the salty air in big, slow gulps.

'My place. Let's go.'

His rough voice was enough to break the spell and she stepped away, rubbing her arms against the sudden cold.

'That might take a while in the buggy,' she said, nodding in its direction.

'Oh,' he said, the single word laden with what would have been comical disappointment if she hadn't felt exactly the same way. 'Well, okay. My place—after we return the *Scoot Car*.'

She shook her head. 'No. It was just the one kiss.'

'What?'

She walked past him, making herself put one foot in front of the other and climb into the buggy rather than stopping and wrapping herself around him again.

She heard the crunch of gravel as he walked around the vehicle. He slid in beside her, his hand resting on the ignition but not turning it.

'What was that, Sophie?'

She couldn't look at him. 'Just a kiss,' she said quickly. 'A moment—like you said. Nothing more.'

'And you think you can stop at just one kiss?' His voice was deep and dangerous in the almost darkness.

'Of course,' she said immediately, firmly and clearly. She had to.

'The offer still stands, Soph. Just say the word.'

'I won't,' she said.

She sensed his smile even though she couldn't see it. 'I wouldn't be so sure.'

CHAPTER EIGHT

Monday 14th November, 9:00 a.m.

From: Sophie Morgan
To: Dan Halliday
Subject: Meeting cancellation
Dan,
The planning meeting on Wednesday is cancelled.
Please refer to the attached notes and map prior to Sunday's barbecue.
I will see you at the bar on Saturday.
Kind regards,
Sophie

Monday 14th November, 9:45 a.m.

Text message from Dan:
Soph, there's no need to be embarrassed. You don't kiss half bad.

Monday 14th November, 9:47 a.m.

Text message from Sophie:
Please confirm that you received my cancellation email.

Monday 14th November, 9:50 a.m.

Text message from Dan:
Received. But I don't remember a planning meeting.
Is our date still on?

Monday 14th November, 9:52 a.m.

Text message from Sophie:
No. There was never a date. It was never real.

FOR the first time in her life Sophie was almost late to work. Not because she was disorganised, or because of bad traffic or anything like that. Simply because it was far easier to drive aimlessly through the streets of Subiaco than to gather up the courage to drive into the wine bar's car park.

Eventually it was the certain knowledge that Dan would never let her forget it if she *was* actually late that finally made her slow down, flick the indicator and turn the steering wheel in the bar's direction. It was only as she dumped her bag in the small staff room that she remembered *never only* had a lifespan of just three more weeks. After that it wouldn't matter. Once the wedding was over she wouldn't see him again.

That should have made her feel better, but it didn't.

And that was bad.

It just wasn't sinking in—no matter how many times she told herself that those long minutes of madness on the beach were simply that: moments. Discrete moments in time that she could now box away and shove to the dustiest recesses of her mind—never to be thought of again.

That wasn't going so well for her.

Instead, her memories of those moments would leap out at her, in full Technicolor, at the most inopportune times. Like at her job interview the other day. Or while trying to think calming *Yes, you can work with him and keep your distance* thoughts on her way to work. Hence her driving about in circles.

It had occurred to her briefly, while twisting herself into knots as she tossed and turned in bed following that incredible kiss, that she could just cancel their agreement.

No risk of any more kisses then!

But it seemed pretty gutless to go down that path. She believed Dan when he said he needed her at the bar, and she wasn't about to let him down. Also, it would totally stuff up her project, and she definitely didn't have time to rustle up a new fake boyfriend in time for the wedding.

And, more importantly, it did seem pretty pathetic that she had so little faith in her self control. If she ended their agreement it would be because she felt she was in real danger of capitulating and becoming the latest in Dan's long line of casual and easily discarded girlfriends.

No, thank you.

So she'd emailed him and cancelled their meeting. *Not* because of the kiss—so she kept telling herself—but because there was no need. If she counted Saturday night as their second date…*no* fake date/planning meeting, well, the project was right on schedule.

She'd also decided to have another crack at the whole 'professional relationship' thing. She'd figured it would make life easier—make sure Dan didn't get the wrong idea or anything—although it had been difficult to maintain when she'd received Dan's text messages. She'd smiled as she'd read them, but had made herself text super-serious messages back—not the flirty, teasing words her fingers had itched to type.

Noticing the wall clock's minute hand tick ever closer to 5:00 p.m., Sophie quickly tied her short black apron around her waist. Taking a deep breath, she straightened her shoulders, eyeing the door with steely determination.

She could do this—walk through that door, act professional.

But before she had the opportunity the door swung open and Dan strode into the room. His height and width made the tiny room even smaller, and she took an involuntary backward step.

'Sophie,' he said by way of greeting, punctuating the word with a curt nod.

'Uh, hi!' Far from her target of 'casual' she could only manage 'oddly high-pitched'.

He walked past her, picking up his jacket from the back of a chair. 'There's an issue at the other bar I need to sort out, so I'll see you tomorrow afternoon?'

She nodded, and seconds later he was gone—back out through the door and into the night.

And that was good, right? That she didn't have to work with him tonight, and that he was finally—after resisting right from the very start—maintaining a professional distance?

It was as if the kiss had never happened—which was exactly what she wanted.

Right?

The argument between two of his more flamboyant chefs took less time to untangle than expected, leaving Dan at an unexpected loose end.

He considered returning to the Subiaco bar, but knew if

he did it would be purely to see Sophie—his new bartender didn't need supervision any more. And somehow he didn't think he'd get a hell of a lot of paperwork done with Sophie mere metres away.

Besides, after her formal email and text messages he'd already decided on his plan of attack—so to speak. Sophie had made it clear that she'd reverted back to her default defensive position: ultra-professional. So he'd go along with that.

For as long as it lasted. Which he really didn't think would be very long at all.

Did Sophie really think they could both stop after just that one kiss?

He didn't. No way.

But Sophie needed to figure that out for herself, and his instincts told him the best way for that to happen was to keep his distance for a while.

With that in mind he made a quick phone call, and promptly invited himself over to his parents' place for dinner. He drove the short distance to their leafy riverside suburb, winding his way through streets liberally populated with opulent mansions—only the occasional modest 1950s home peeking out amongst the triple garages, glass-edged balconies and angular architectural 'features'.

Unlike Sophie, he hadn't grown up in the house where his parents now lived. That elegant but much smaller house had been a few suburbs away. Over the years, as his parents' legal practice had grown, so had the size of their home. Likewise its location had become even more fashionable with every move. Now, in retirement, they lived in crazily expensive and crazily picturesque Peppermint Grove, in an oversized home complete with river glimpses.

It was a great place—no question—but a tiny part of Dan kind of liked how Sophie still got to sleep in her old room. It was a nice idea—growing up in just the one house, maybe one day bringing your own kids over for sleepovers with their grandmother…

What?

He parked his car on the furthest edge of the curved driveway and took great pains to erase *that* unwanted little daydream. It had been years—*years*—since he'd painted such fanciful pictures in his mind.

Surely by now he should have got it through his thick skull that daydreams like that were as fragile and insubstantial as the head on a pint of beer?

He shoved the car door open and climbed out just as his mother opened the front door.

'Dan! Hi!'

He leapt up the sandstone steps to the doorway two at a time, grinning when he saw his mother's Saturday evening attire.

'Looking lovely in your aqua velour tracksuit tonight, Mum,' he said, earning himself a dazzling smile.

She propped a hand on her slightly plump hip and struck a runway model pose. 'Oh, this old thing?'

He laughed, and she stood on her tiptoes to kiss his cheek.

Dan followed her inside, through the high-ceilinged hallway and past the professionally decorated front rooms. In the open plan kitchen/dining room his dad sat at their curved glass table—'It's a statement piece, darling,' his mother had explained once—surrounded by small mountains of manila folders and lakes of scattered white paper.

'Enjoying retirement there, Dad?' he asked, taking the seat across from him.

His dad looked up, brushing his shaggy grey-streaked hair out of his eyes. 'It's an interesting case,' his dad offered by way of explanation—as he always did.

He asked his dad questions about the case as his mum prepared dinner, and later helped relocate the landscape of paperwork to the study. This elicited much muttering from his mother about the most appropriate original location for said paperwork, and his dad swiftly countered by saying that he much preferred to be near her when he worked. This earned his dad the biggest beef-and-rice-stuffed capsicum and an extra dollop of creamy mashed potato, all swimming in homemade tomato sauce. It was Dan's favourite of the traditional Croatian dishes his mum regularly made.

'Do you ever miss it?' his mother asked as they all mopped up the remains of their dinner with crusty bread.

Knowing exactly what she meant, he got straight to the point. 'I'm not and will never be a lawyer again, Mum.'

'But you were interested in your dad's case.'

He nodded, familiar with this conversation and frustrated that they were having it yet again. 'I was. But that doesn't mean I want to change careers.'

Right on cue, his dad chimed in. 'Such a shame—top of your class and everything.' He even shook his head in bemusement.

'Do we need to discuss this again?' He couldn't even get annoyed with them, as he knew they came from a position of genuine confusion rather than outright disapproval. They were proud of the wine bar's success, in their own way, but not in the same way they'd been when he'd got into law, or when he'd graduated, or got his first job.

They were also convinced—although maybe just slightly wavering after all these years—that he was just 'in a phase'. Still recovering from the horrendous mess that had been the end of his short marriage. But he was far from that empty shell he'd been when Amalie had left him.

He had countless regrets from that period of his life, but as far as he was concerned buying the bars was one of the few things he'd got right. It had been the best thing he'd ever done for himself, with the only ongoing fly in the ointment

being his parents' disappointment. They missed the obses-
sively focussed uni student who had talked so excitedly about
one day following in their footsteps and running their practice himself.

He didn't.

His dad stacked their plates and carried them to the
kitchen while his mum studied him across the table. He had
her to thank for his olive skin and almost black hair, but she
watched him with hazel eyes, so different from the pale blue
of his father's and his own.

'Nina's pregnant again,' she said. 'She'll be due in May—
isn't that great?'

He smiled, genuinely thrilled for his young cousin. 'That's
great news. I'll give her a call this week.'

His mum nodded slowly, and the atmosphere—which
hadn't really recovered from the awkwardness of the law
conversation—went all off-kilter again. He braced himself
for the inevitable question.

'So…are you seeing anyone at the moment?'

He had to laugh at her transparent attempt at casualness.

'I think next time I come to dinner I'll just confirm my
commitment to my current career and my single status the
moment I walk in the door.'

His dad laughed from behind him as he stacked the dishwasher. 'Please do. It would save your mother some angst.'

His mum shot a glare in the direction of the kitchen. 'I do
not angst.' She sniffed. 'I just care.'

And she still harboured hope of the future appearance
of miniature Dan Hallidays. He was eternally gratefully
that he'd restrained himself from blurting out the fact of
Amalie's pregnancy all those years ago. It would have killed
his mum to know just how close she'd been to becoming a
grandmother.

And he absolutely mustn't tell her about that silly little daydream he'd had about Sophie.

No, not *Sophie*. About a hypothetical woman whose mother hypothetically still lived in the family home.

Definitely *not* Sophie.

His mother was looking at him in a funny way, her head tilted at an angle. 'Hang on. Dan—you *are* seeing someone, aren't you?'

He met her curious gaze with steady, emotionless eyes. 'No, I'm not.'

'Oh, he *is*!' his mum said, and all but clapped her hands in delight. 'Tell me—who is she?'

Dan's jaw clenched.

His dad returned to the table, slapping him on the shoulder as he passed by. 'Good job, son. Tell us all about the lucky lady.'

'There isn't one to talk about.'

His parents shared a long look, and then turned back to him with matching knowing grins.

He couldn't even be bothered arguing any more. They'd made up their minds—why and how, he had no idea.

'I'm so pleased for you, darling,' his mum said, reaching out and grabbing his hand.

'There's no need to start planning the wedding, Mum. It's nothing serious.'

He wasn't sure why he'd confirmed Sophie's existence. Possibly a misguided hope that doing so might defuse the situation—making it clear that it was a purely short-term arrangement.

He'd been wrong. His words had simply ratcheted up that enthusiasm. He shouldn't have said anything. It was cruel to get his parents' hopes up. Their marriage—and marriage itself—was so important to them.

As it had once been equally important to him.

He must have been the only guy in Perth under twenty-five who'd dated women with the end goal of marriage. But then it had all been part of his plan—that pretty painting he'd had in his mind. Degree, job, house, marriage, babies…

He'd seen it, so crystal clear, his picture-book definition of success.

His huge mistake had been tackling each task with the same close-minded focus that had elicited his high marks and his brilliant straight-out-of-university career. The ideal attitude for work—the worst for marriage.

And he hadn't even been close to realising that until it was far too late.

His mum was still watching him with a beaming smile, wedding confetti practically shining in her eyes.

But his dad, also silently observing him, wore a totally different expression. He watched Dan with concern and contemplation, the gears ticking over in his mind plain to see. He finally spoke. 'You know, Dan, one day you'll need to forgive yourself. It's never just one person's fault when a marriage ends.'

His mum blinked, surprised by the statement, but then nodded and smiled at him with encouragement. As if he was supposed to suddenly burst out with, *Yes, you're absolutely right! It wasn't my fault that my marriage collapsed and I didn't notice until the moment my wife walked out the door. Thank you. I'm cured! I'll go get married and have your grandchildren tomorrow.*

He was being unfair, he knew.

Because, of course, his parents didn't know the full story.

CHAPTER NINE

The Sophie Project 2.1 (Project Manager: S. Morgan)
Task Four: The Second Date (cancelled)
Task Five: Emma's Barbecue

EVEN though they were right on time for the Sunday evening barbecue, the number of cars crowding the lawn and street meant they needed to park some distance away. Dan effortlessly lifted the Esky out of the back of her mum's hatchback—the same Esky Sophie had dragged and hauled into the car with much difficulty before picking him up. If nothing else, a fake boyfriend was super-convenient when it came to the lifting and shifting of heavy objects.

They began to walk down the hill towards Emma's house, shaded by the vast jacarandas that dotted the footpath with blue and purple flowers. They walked in the same silence they'd maintained during the drive after their polite, stilted conversation had completely dried up. Sophie kept her gaze straight ahead, terribly aware of the man beside her and the jumble of delicious sensations his closeness triggered: a shiver whenever they accidentally touched, liquid warmth in her belly whenever she looked at his lips.

'Sophie, slow down.'

His hand on her arm stilled her instantly, and she made herself shrug away from his touch.

'Why?'

He pushed his sunglasses onto his head, meeting her eyes with his clear blue gaze. 'Have you forgotten why I'm here? About the project?'

She shook her head. 'Of course not.'

He raised an eyebrow. 'You sure? Because last time I checked a woman in love doesn't stalk ahead of her boyfriend as if he doesn't exist.'

She tugged at the strapless neckline of her blue-and-grey maxi-dress. He did have a point. 'Maybe we just had a fight?'

He grinned. 'Sure—if that's the image you were going for. I thought it was more "blissfully happy", but we can go with "utterly miserable" if that's what you'd prefer.'

She bit the inside of her lip to stop herself returning his smile.

'Fine. I'll stop stalking.'

'Good news,' he said, and they continued on their way. Sauntering, not stalking.

Three houses before their destination Dan caught her hand, lacing his fingers with hers deliberately.

She stiffened, but with other couples approaching the house from the opposite direction made no move to extract her hand.

'Is this *really* necessary?' she whispered.

He leant close, his breath hot against her ear. 'What do you think?'

No, it's not.

But for some reason, rather than saying the words, she let the tension ease from her arm and shoulder and just kept on holding his hand.

Because it would help the 'blissfully happy' image, of course.

She darted a glance up at Dan, expecting a raised eyebrow or a smug expression. She saw neither—just his kissable lips kicked up in the sexiest of smiles. And there were all sorts of promises swirling about in his knowing gaze.

She just had to say the word.

Sophie looked away.

Their hands fell apart as they negotiated the narrow steps to the front door, but not before Emma—standing at the threshold to welcome the steady stream of guests—had seen them. Emma's eyebrows were raised in completely unsubtle interest during their short introductions, disappearing further into her choppy blond fringe when Sophie managed to utter the all-important words: 'This is my boyfriend, Dan.'

Dan went ahead of them into the house, and Emma grabbed Sophie's arm before she could follow him.

'Where on earth did you find *him*?' she asked, her eyes following Dan's jean-clad butt down the hallway. 'You've been back in Perth for, what? Five minutes? And you've managed to unearth *that*?'

'Speed dating,' she said simply. 'I recommend it.'

As Dan disappeared around the corner Emma dragged her attention back to Sophie. 'I'll have to give it a try some time.'

Sophie laughed. 'Emma, you're married.'

She shrugged, her eyes sparkling. 'Surely it's okay if I only go for the view?' She paused, shaking her head. 'Far out, Soph. That guy is one hell of a way to forget about Rick.'

For once Rick's name didn't trigger some visceral reaction. No bottomless ache, no stabbing pain. Nothing.

So she smiled broadly, unable to resist her old friend's enthusiasm. 'Yeah,' she said, 'I know.'

It had been a long time since Dan had taken a woman to a barbecue. Or, more accurately, had a woman take *him* to a barbecue. The women he dated figured out pretty quickly that he wasn't going to invite them to dinner with his friends or get-togethers with his mates, and certainly not to any family events. For some women this didn't matter. For the ones to whom it did—who decided that they wanted more than something fun and mutually satisfying—well, it was at that realisation that they generally walked. And that worked fine for him.

So it was strange to be at this barbecue with Sophie—to be 'the boyfriend' again. He'd expected the strangeness, of course. But not absolutely hating it was the real surprise. Even though it was all fake, he'd still expected it to feel unequivocally *wrong*—in the same way the very idea of being in a relationship felt wrong to him.

He wouldn't go so far as to say it felt *right*, though. Having Sophie introduce him to friends as her boyfriend, and the subsequent small talk he engaged in about how they'd met and so on—well, that was all a bit weird, of course. But it was working. He'd lost count of the number of people who told him how *thrilled* they were that Sophie had moved on from her broken engagement.

And, if he was really honest with himself, he could think of a lot worse ways to spend his Sunday evening than sitting in a lovely back garden on a plastic folding chair next to Sophie, sausages and potluck salads piled onto the paper plates on their laps.

Earlier, as he'd held her hand on the footpath, she'd relaxed—just a little—and the awkward tightness of her body had softened before him. But more than a flicker of wariness still danced in her eyes—on the few occasions she'd met his gaze, at least.

Holding her hand had been a diversion from his game plan, no matter which way he looked at it. Part of the fake boyfriend show? Maybe—if he completely ignored the fact that he was hardly the type of guy to consider public handholding essential boyfriend behaviour. He knew what it had been—a not exactly subtle excuse to touch her.

So, yeah, not really consistent with the 'keeping his distance' plan. But hardly worthy of regret—and besides, it hadn't escaped his notice that when he touched Sophie she was several orders of magnitude less sensible. Instead she was more natural, more…uninhibited.

Possibly a state of mind he should be pursuing more vigorously…

She leant over and whispered in his ear, 'Thank you for tonight. You're playing this perfectly.'

'I don't know,' he said, the cogs in his brain turning over efficiently as inspiration struck. 'Do you think we've put on enough of a show?'

She considered his question seriously, her forehead crinkling. 'What do you think?'

He shook his head solemnly. 'We could do better.'

She chewed on her bottom lip. 'What should we do?'

He leant just a little bit closer—close enough to smell the vanilla of her perfume. 'I think what we're doing right now is a good start. Is anyone watching?'

Her gaze flickered away from him. 'Yes. A few people. Karen is. You remember—the bride-to-be?'

'That's perfect, right?'

'Yeah. So what do we do?'

'I could kiss you—'

'*No.*'

Far more than just a flicker of wariness in *that* look. More like a *Don't even think about it, buddy!* glare.

Well, it had been worth a try. 'Are we back to the kissing rules?'

She inclined her head slightly. 'Yes, definitely.'

'So I guess putting my hand on your knee is off limits, too?'

She glowered at him. But he didn't miss the merest hint of a grin shaping the corners of her lips.

'There you go—whispering and sharing a private joke. How much more in love could we get?'

Her gaze dropped downwards for a moment, before slowly creeping up again. Ah, he recognised this expression—Sophie in perfectionist project manager mode. 'Maybe you *should* kiss me,' she said, as matter-of-fact as if she was talking about the weather. Then, with a pointed, no-nonsense look, 'On the cheek, of course.'

'Of course,' he said. If she wanted to pretend this was just about her project, that was one hundred percent fine with him.

Despite her businesslike words there was barely a gap between them. They'd both crept ever nearer as they'd talked, drawn together like magnets.

All he had to do was shift his weight forward, dip his head slightly to the side, and his lips would brush her skin. But he took his time.

He inhaled her subtle scent. He silently acknowledged the moment her project manager mask slipped and a blush warmed her delicate skin. And he smiled as she shivered at the touch of his breath on her cheek.

Then, finally, he kissed her.

It wasn't enough. And it was a million times worse than when he'd last kissed her cheek, as this time he knew exactly what he was missing out on.

He straightened. Cleared his throat.

'How was that?' he asked, picking up his plastic fork and stabbing at a piece of potato salad.

'Very convincing,' she said, her voice brisk but just the tiniest bit uneven. 'I don't think anyone would ever think it was fake.'

He nodded.

This whole charade would be a hell of a lot easier if it didn't feel so real.

* * *

'Sorry to interrupt you two lovebirds!'

It was Emma, her bubbly enthusiasm snapping Sophie out of whatever off-balance, dreamy place Dan's chaste kiss had sent her to. She'd been diligently slicing up her sausage, and it was only at Emma's voice that she realised she'd reduced it to dozens of tiny inedible pieces.

She put her plate under her seat, hidden by the skirt of her full-length dress.

'Do you need some help, Emma?' she asked, adding hopefully, 'In the kitchen?'

Some distance from Dan was just what she needed. *Twice* now she'd let down her guard—when she'd held his hand and now with their kiss. No matter which way she spun it—both were utterly unnecessary. Dressing it up as part of the project was just lying to herself.

'Don't be silly. You're a guest. I just wanted to let you know that it's time to start warming up those vocal cords!'

Oh, no.

'Sophie sings?' Dan asked with obvious interest.

'I don't,' Sophie answered quickly, just as Emma said, 'Oh, yes, she does!'

'I don't believe it,' Dan said.

'You'll see,' Emma said happily. 'Brad bought me a karaoke machine for my birthday!'

Sophie all but shuddered in horror as Emma sashayed away.

'I'm going to need a drink,' she muttered, getting to her feet.

Minutes and a few liberal mouthfuls of Verdelho later, she didn't feel any better. She returned to her seat in the corner of Emma's large paved patio. Dan watched with laughing eyes as she approached.

'*This* I have got to see,' he said. 'I never would have picked you as the karaoke type.'

'You were right. I'm not. Emma is referring to a short period in my *un*wild and *un*crazy youth when I may have made some dubious decisions with the assistance of copious amounts of alcohol.'

'Decisions involving singing in public?'

'Sadly, yes. Although—in my defence—I was always a backup singer. Karen and Emma would share the lead.'

Her two old friends were excitedly setting up the karaoke machine beneath a porch light that acted conveniently like a spotlight. A spotlight she had absolutely *no* intention of standing in.

Unfortunately she had very little say in the matter, and soon found herself exercising her dreadful singing voice as Emma's—very quiet—backup singer.

'So singing lessons were never on one of your to-do lists, then?' Dan asked as she returned to her seat.

'Very funny,' she said. 'I did warn you.'

He just grinned at her.

As the night wore on and nearly every other guest was dragged into the spotlight—all with various degrees of success—Sophie's mortification faded. Guests soon made the patio a dance floor, spinning and bouncing around to everything from heavy metal to nineties boy band to power ballads.

She and Dan didn't dance—not because she didn't want to, but because she wasn't silly enough to put herself in a position where there were even more legitimate opportunities to touch each other. Dan's occasionally boyfriendish arm around her shoulder or waist as they chatted with other guests was already doing her in—she couldn't handle it if they were on the dance floor and something slow suddenly came on.

If she found herself pressed against Dan again, arms wrapped around each other just like they were at the beach— well, she had a terrible feeling that any self-control or sensible note to self would be hurled out of the metaphorical window.

So when a slow dance *did* come on they were standing together, the couple they'd been talking to having added themselves to the sea of swaying bodies the instant the first familiar bars were played.

Karen's fiancé Ben was at the microphone, but before he'd even sung the first word of the song Sophie's feet had begun to shuffle even as her heart plummeted.

She moved without volition—the helpless Pavlovian result of months and months of practice.

Practising in the Surrey Hills dance studio near her house. Practising in her lounge room with the coffee table shoved up against the sofa.

Feet moving, hands guiding, bodies swaying—Rick and her laughing.

It was their wedding song.

She closed her eyes, taking deep, deep breaths, battling against the waves of unexpected and unwanted emotion that flooded over her.

Tears of frustration stung her eyes. She'd thought she'd finally started to move on—that Rick no longer had the power to hurt her.

'Sophie, are you okay?' She could barely hear Dan. The song's verses seemed many times magnified as they echoed through her skull, her bones and her heart.

She didn't respond, just busied her rogue feet with the act of walking into the house and out onto Emma's front yard. She shouldn't still be able to hear the song, but it followed her, repeating itself over and over in her head.

What she was feeling wasn't about Rick at all, she realised. No, instead the song was like a soundtrack to a time in her life when everything had been perfect. When a man had loved her for exactly who she was and hadn't given a damn that she wasn't some package deal. A time when she'd

believed that her infertility really didn't matter. Not at all.
That she was enough.

And it had all been a lie.

She *hadn't* been enough for Rick.

And this song—this song she'd once loved—wouldn't let
her lie to herself any more.

Maybe she'd never be enough for anyone.

Dan caught her hand as she charged down the driveway.
'Sophie. *Stop.*'

She wrenched her hand free, using far more force than
necessary. 'I have to go.' And she kept right on walking
away—away from that song and, she hoped, the emptiness
inside her. She broke into an awkward jog, her flat leather
sandals slapping like gunshots on the footpath.

Dan effortlessly overtook her, blocking her escape route
with his body. He didn't touch her again, just stood there.

Sophie realised the song was gone. Now she could hear her
uneven breathing—the only sound in the deserted dark street.

'Do you want to tell me what's going on?'

She shook her head. How could she possibly explain?

'No, not good enough, Soph,' he said, his voice firm. 'It
was that song, right? As soon as it started you shut down.'

'It was my wedding song,' she said brusquely. 'You
know—the first dance as a married couple? It just brought
up some bad memories, that's all. I was just being silly.'

Dan didn't buy her *I'm all fine now* tone, she could tell.

'Sophie?' It was a woman's voice, low and concerned,
behind her. Emma.

Oh, God, she'd just made a total fool of herself.

She turned and faced a worried-looking Emma. 'I'm sorry,
Em. I just needed some fresh air.'

It was a good indicator of their long lasting friendship,
even if they had rarely seen each other in the past few years,

that Emma didn't point out that there was plenty of fresh air in her backyard.

'Are you okay?' Her gaze flicked to Dan over Sophie's shoulder.

No. 'Yes,' she said. 'But we might head off now, I think. I have a job interview first thing tomorrow.'

Emma nodded reluctantly. 'Let's catch up for a coffee soon, okay?' she said as she retreated back to the house.

'I'll just go grab the Esky and your bag,' Dan said, following Emma inside.

Sophie leant against the trunk of a jacaranda, watching them walk up the stairs and then seeing the fly screen slam behind them.

She hadn't even had her bag—or her car keys. Where exactly had she thought she was going?

Away.

But that, of course, was the problem. The emptiness inside her couldn't be escaped—the inability to start her getaway vehicle notwithstanding.

Even her project plan couldn't fix it. So what if she'd decided to tell every prospective boyfriend that she was infertile? What would that achieve, really?

It would just accelerate the inevitable.

Disappointment.

Meaningless words meant to reassure.

Then rejection. Always rejection.

Even her relationships before Rick—before her boyfriends had hit an age when children were high on their to-do lists—had been temporary. There had always been an unspoken, underlying understanding that she was not a woman men chose to settle down with. She'd known it. And then Rick had made her believe that she'd had it all wrong, and she'd revelled in what she now knew was a lie.

The type of man she wanted—a man who'd propose marriage and a home and a life together—why would *he* want her?

Dan—a man who was the antithesis of the man she wanted—walked back towards her, empty Esky bouncing against his leg. She drank him in as he walked, backlit by the light on Emma's front porch.

Broad shoulders, lean hips, long legs.

And he wanted *her*. Suddenly the fact that he came with an expiry date didn't matter. The pull—the *connection*—between them was so strong that resisting him already felt like a battle she would never win. So why resist? Why not stop all her over-thinking and justifications and sensible decisions and just let go? Give in to this unfamiliar spectacular spark and let herself experience what her body so badly wanted? What *she* so badly wanted? And what now felt like the most natural, most perfect, most necessary thing in the world?

Then in three weeks he'd be gone, and she'd never need to tell him she was broken inside.

She met his eyes, pouring all the pain and frustration and *need* she felt into her gaze. He stopped dead, his grip on the Esky's handle failing. It fell onto the grass with a thud. And then, without a word, he walked to where she stood, still propped against the tree. Her bag landed at her feet and his hands pressed flat against the jacaranda's trunk on either side of face.

His eyes hadn't shifted from hers, but she could see the question in his gaze.

She swallowed. 'This isn't about my project plan, or about you trying to make me more spontaneous or something, okay? This isn't me saying "the word", or whatever you called it.'

He nodded.

'This is about *me* wanting *you*.' His eyes glinted in the moonlight. 'And *you* wanting…*me*.'

It took everything she had not to look away or to blush. But she managed it, keeping their gazes locked together as he leant towards her, right up until she felt his breath hot against her lips. A split second before his mouth covered hers her eyes slid shut.

And then he kissed her. No preliminaries this time, just demanding, determined and sure. The touch of his tongue made her shiver and sent her hands from her sides to his waist.

She was deliciously hemmed in, with his palms still flat against the bark, so without the option of threading her hands into his hair, like before, this time she made do with exploring the shape of his back.

It was far from a hardship to run her fingers along his muscular ridges and planes through his shirt, or to drag her nails down his spine, halting only when her fingers hit the leather of his belt.

He kissed her expertly, passionately and voraciously, as if she was something special, and as if he couldn't get enough of her. He tasted crisp and clean, with a hint of cinnamon from the apple crumble they'd both had for dessert.

She sighed when he settled his weight against her, and he groaned into her mouth when she gave in to temptation and snuck her fingers under the hem of his T-shirt. His skin was warm and smooth—and far too covered in clothing. She pushed the fabric upwards, barely aware of what she was doing.

Dan's hands fell to her waist and she tensed in anticipation, wanting to feel his hands on her. All over her.

But then his mouth backed off from hers—and then completely away when she automatically followed him with her lips.

His body was still tight against her, and she dipped her

hands into the valley at the small of his back and pressed him even closer against her. His hardness to her heat.

'Hell, Soph,' he said, low and dangerous. 'We can't do this here.'

She knew she should feel embarrassed, but she didn't. It should also have shocked her that her first instinct was to tell him *Don't stop*.

But luckily, somehow—despite the way her body thrummed with anticipation—a small part of her normal sensible self was able to force her hands from Dan's back and coherent, rational words from her mouth.

'Your place. Now.'

CHAPTER TEN

THE necessary frustration of returning her mother's car and leaving a note on the kitchen counter—all the while thanking her lucky stars that her mum was sleeping—was considerably offset during the too long taxi drive to Dan's house. They sat quite respectably, on either side of the back seat—nothing for the driver to see during his frequent glances in the rear vision mirror.

But Dan held her hand, drawing gorgeous little circles and swirls with his fingers on the sensitive skin of her wrist. It was so innocent, but the sensations it set off like fireworks inside her were anything but.

Finally, outside his townhouse, Dan all but dragged her from the footpath to his front door, kissing her even as he turned the key in the lock. They spilled inside, the door slamming shut and then both of their bodies slamming against it. Their mouths came together almost violently in their quest to become ever closer, lips grazing teeth, tongues tangling.

Sophie's hands started right where they'd left off, catching the hem of his T-shirt and shoving it upwards with steady determination. They broke apart while Dan pulled the fabric over his head, but they were back together before it hit the floor.

Her hands skimmed over his back, and then around and

over his chest. He was all firm, hard, hot skin, only a few hairs smattering his torso.

Dan's clever hands explored her, too, following the shape of her hips and waist. He took big handfuls of her dress, until the fabric was bunched at her waist and her naked legs were rubbing against his roughness of his jeans.

And then his mouth lifted from hers.

'No…' she whispered, and she felt him smile against her jaw.

Her hands raced to his hair, to tug him back to her lips, but he ignored her, pressing hot, slow kisses beneath her ear, down her neck, along her collarbone. She let her head fall back against the door as he continued his leisurely journey, her body a luscious juxtaposition of ever-increasing tension and languorous, liquid heat.

'You're just perfect,' he said roughly.

The words felt almost as good as his touch.

And then his strong arms caught her beneath the knees and he swung her up into his arms.

Automatically her arms tightened around his neck, and she tried to meet his eyes in the darkness.

'Are you serious?' she said. 'I'm too heavy.'

Although he made her feel light as a feather.

He carried her effortlessly past a flight of stairs and into a bedroom, depositing her gently beside the bed.

'Pay attention, Soph,' he said, the moonlight revealing the heat and intensity in his gaze. 'You're perfect.'

Early-morning light poked through gaps in the wooden blinds, painting Dan's body with slivers and dapples of sunshine. Sophie ran her finger along the curve of his back, tracing every dot and stripe. Some softly, some harder, and some with the gentle scrape of her nails.

'Good morning to you, too,' he said, sleepy and husky and sexy as hell.

He rolled over, propping himself up on an elbow. Now she could properly see the body she'd had so much fun exploring, and it looked exactly as it felt—powerful, smooth and lean. Not over-inflated muscle on muscle, just hard-angled strength—from his beautifully broad shoulders all the way down to his toes.

Not even a sheet covered them. The bedcovers had been kicked off, or more likely were just a casualty from all the fun they'd been having.

He was studying her, too, his gaze heavy-lidded and as admiring as when he'd first seen her naked skin. No one had ever looked at her like this, with such shiver-inducing intensity. Under his gaze she didn't think to feel modest, or to suck in her stomach, or to catalogue her flaws. In fact, when he was looking at her she forgot she even had them.

She reached for him, her index finger circling a perfect sphere of light on his breastbone. He reached for her, his hand moving in a gentle caress from the curve of her hip to the dip of her waist.

So what happened now? How did one go about having a no-strings-attached, who-cares-about-the-future, living-in-the-moment fling?

Were there rules? A handshake?

Dan's eyes met hers, almost grey in the filtered light. 'I can see you thinking,' he said. The pad of his finger outlined the creases in her forehead. 'And here,' he said, his finger drifting downwards to where she'd sucked her bottom lip subconsciously between her teeth, brushing against her and then away.

She released her lip, running her tongue over the spot where he'd so briefly touched her.

His gaze darkened.

'You're welcome to distract me,' she said.

And he was kissing her almost before the words had left her mouth.

'Dan!'

Sophie's voice was loud and harsh—and far from the beautifully sleep-fuzzed whisper of a few hours earlier. He sat up, shaking his own foggy head, to find Sophie out of bed, still naked, doing a commendable impression of a headless chicken. She picked up his jeans before tossing them aside. Then did the same to his shirt, before scurrying out of the bedroom—to where, he had no idea.

'What are you looking for?' he called out, rubbing his bleary eyes.

'The *time*,' she said, her tone now unquestionably panicky. 'Who doesn't have a bedside clock, anyway?'

He could hear the urgent smack of her bare feet against his hardwood floors as he hauled himself out of bed, tugging his boxer shorts on quickly.

'I use my phone as an alarm,' he said, trying to remember where he'd left it.

He heard a frustrated groan. 'I cannot *believe* you don't even have the time set on your microwave. What is wrong with you?' A pause, then a muttered, '*Where* did I put my handbag?'

He spotted his phone on the floor, where it must have fallen from his pocket, just as he heard a shriek from his living room.

'Oh, my God! It's half past nine!'

He walked out of his bedroom to see Sophie, a look of horror on her face, standing in the long rectangles of sunlight thrown by the frosted glass panels of his front door. The contents of her handbag were scattered at her feet and she held her phone out to him in abject despair, as if by taking it from her hands he could somehow turn back time.

'Your interview,' he said, understanding finally dawning.

'Yes,' she said. 'At ten.'

'In the city?'

She nodded.

'Well, hurry up, then. I'll get you there in time.'

Her jaw actually dropped, and she stared at him for long, confused moments.

'Pardon me?'

'It's ten minutes' drive from here. You'll get there easy.'

'Easy?' she repeated. 'But my suit is at my mum's. Twenty minutes away. I'll never make it back in time.'

He shrugged. 'You'll just have to wear what you wore last night.'

'What I wore last night?'

'Unless you'd prefer to cancel your interview?'

She shook her head. 'No, that would be even worse.'

'So it's decided, then?'

She rubbed her forehead. 'Oh, God—yes, I guess it is.'

'Shower's that way,' he said, pointing down the hallway.

She padded towards the bathroom as he admired her rear view. He supposed it was a little heartless to check her out when she was in the midst of such a momentously shocking occasion: *Sophie Morgan was running late.* But really he had no choice in the matter. Looking at Sophie was a compulsion. It had been long before last night.

'I don't suppose you have any make-up stashed away somewhere?' she said, not sounding even a little bit hopeful.

'Sorry,' he said. 'All out.'

'I don't *believe* this,' she said, just before he heard the hiss of running water.

Ten minutes later they were in Dan's car, Sophie dabbing

at a just-discovered tomato sauce mark on her dress with a damp teatowel.

'I don't believe this,' she repeated. 'This is a disaster.'

He didn't comment, deciding that keeping his mouth shut was probably the best way to go, given the tension radiating off Sophie in waves.

'You think this is funny, don't you?' she said.

'No,' he said, figuring the single word was relatively safe.

Apparently not. 'You *do*! You think this is good for me— being late for something.'

'Of course not. Being late to a job interview is not something I'd wish on anyone. Particularly you.'

She fell back into her seat and blew out a long, frustrated sigh. 'Sorry,' she said. 'That was unfair.' And they fell into awkward silence.

Now that he'd had a shower and his brain had finally started to kick into a gear that could think beyond a naked Sophie walking around his house, he was getting a little tense himself.

What was going on here? His standard *modus operandi* the morning after was to get up early—requiring setting his alarm, which he had obviously forgotten—and then take the lady in question to breakfast at his favourite café in Subiaco. It was a good plan on two fronts: 1. He loved a good breakfast, complete with bacon, sausages and other artery-clogging delights, and 2. It circumvented the dangerous illusion of intimacy waking up together in bed inevitably created.

But he had let himself wake up with Sophie and he'd liked it. A lot. And, even worse, after they'd made love it hadn't even occurred to him to get out of bed. No, instead they'd fallen asleep again in each other's arms.

In. Each. Other's. Arms.

Was that really a good idea, given Sophie's predisposition for long-term meaningful relationships? What was she going to think? That it was more than just one night together?

Was it more than one night together?

Yes, probably. He'd suggested a fling—it felt like for ever ago—and that was most likely what she was intending. Or maybe not. *No*, just one night—just as she'd said it was only that one unbelievable kiss on the beach after the sunset.

Did it matter? Did he care?

It shouldn't. He shouldn't.

The effort to not care was making his muscles bunch and his jaw tighten uncomfortably.

Sophie cleared her throat. 'Thank you for driving me in. And for being so calm when I'm being a psychotic hot mess.'

Hot, yes. The rest, well—that was just Sophie. He got it. Running late to an interview must feel like the end of the world to her.

He also didn't feel calm. He felt confused. On edge.

He nodded tightly.

'You should feel pretty proud of yourself, really,' she said. 'For distracting me enough that I forgot about my alarm. About the interview, actually.'

He couldn't help but smile. 'I can't apologise for that,' he said.

'You shouldn't,' she said softly.

They fell into silence again, but it had a different essence this time.

'Ah...' she said finally. 'Um...are there any guidelines or something else I should know about for this?'

'For what?' he said, shooting a quick glance at her before returning his attention to the still heavy morning traffic.

Her head was down as she fiddled with the teatowel in her lap.

'You know—*us*.'

'Us?' he said, far more severely than he'd intended. Habit,

maybe. An automatic reaction to a woman connecting herself to him in such a way.

She laughed without a hint of humour. '*Wow.* Way to panic, Dan. I just meant—you know—our fling. Or whatever it is.'

The car slid to a stop at a red light. The high rise venue for her interview was only a minute or two away.

He didn't know what to say. He was still processing his body's unexpected reaction, its sudden release of tension from his jaw through to his toes. He'd all but sagged in relief at the knowledge that Sophie wanted more than a single night together. And his relief bothered him. A lot.

The light went green and he still hadn't spoken. He could see Sophie out of the corner of his eye—fidgeting, bouncing her knees. Maybe about the interview. Maybe about what he was going to say. He pressed his foot to the accelerator and the car continued towards their destination.

He still didn't know what to say.

Should he just end this now? Before it went any further? Before it got even more complicated? He didn't like how he was feeling right now. As if his world had been knocked off-balance.

He nosed the car into a loading bay—the only possible place to drop her off on the sardine-packed CBD street. He couldn't park there, of course, so he kept the motor running, searching for words that stubbornly evaded him.

Sophie opened the door, her action almost violent, then twisted and leapt out of her seat in a stiff, ungraceful movement. She stuck her head back into the car to snatch up her handbag.

'Thanks for the lift,' she said, her voice tight.

'Sophie, I—'

She met his eyes. Raised her eyebrows. The only make-up she wore was a moisturiser she'd unearthed in the bowels of his bathroom cupboard—a misguided gift from his mother, he suspected. Yet she was still beautiful. Dark, dark blue eyes, porcelain skin, rose coloured lips that tasted just as gorgeous as they looked.

She squeezed her eyes shut. Shook her head rapidly once, twice.

When her eyes reopened they were cool.

Then she straightened, slammed the door, and was gone—her gauzy summery dress swallowed up by a footpath awash with starched shirts and pinstriped suits.

All things considered, the interview went remarkably well. And there were a heck of a lot of things *to* consider. Her clothes, for one. So, *so* inappropriate for an interview. And she didn't think she'd ever stop cringing at the memory of the Managing Director's expression when he'd noticed her purpley-black-painted toenails. *Ugh.*

No make-up, for another. Now, she'd never considered herself particularly vain. Not the type to wear a full face of make-up to the supermarket on a Saturday morning, for example. But she'd *never* gone to work without wearing make-up. She wouldn't say it was like armour, or anything dramatic like that, it just made her look good. Professional. Polished. And she liked that.

So, not surprisingly, without make-up she felt like an unprofessional ragamuffin.

But really, once she'd got past a heartfelt apology for her appearance, she could put aside the way she looked, because she couldn't do a single thing to fix it. She was on time, she was otherwise well prepared for the interview, and that was that.

Unfortunately she couldn't put aside the ache inside her. *That* was what made the interview remarkable—the fact that she managed to conduct the entire thing like a rational, intelligent human being.

And not like the very, very stupid person she felt like.

After the interview she visited the company's bathroom and stared at herself for what felt like ages in the unforgiving fluorescent lit mirror.

What had Dan seen when their eyes had met? When she'd been standing on the footpath as stiff as a board and he'd been sprawled, casual as you like, in his luxurious leather seat?

Had he seen the fraud she suspected she was?

Oh, under the jacaranda tree it had all been about the *want*, about the *need*. But in the morning, when he'd looked at her as if she was something exquisite, caressed her as if he would never get enough, she'd bought it. All of it.

Stupid. *So* stupid.

She'd been happy to settle for a fling, knowing deep down that it was all he was capable of.

But he didn't even want that. She'd had the most incredible night of her life, and he was going to discard her as if it was nothing.

Well, not *as if* it was nothing. It must have *been* nothing to him.

Nothing? *Really?* Did she really believe that?

She studied her face: the smattering of freckles she normally hid beneath make-up, the tired smudges beneath her eyes. She didn't look great. It was a fact.

But in the car just before, when their gazes had caught and hung for an age, she'd known—*known*—that he hadn't been comparing her to the bevy of beauties she was sure he was accustomed to. He'd been looking at *her*, connecting with *her*.

Last night hadn't been nothing. She was sure of it.

But the one thing she was even more certain of was that he wasn't going to do a thing about it. She'd seen the moment he'd mentally slammed the door on any chance of more between them. He'd probably seen the stupid stars in her eyes and it had frightened him.

Something—his ex-wife, maybe—*something* had damaged him.

She'd walked away before he'd had the chance to speak. She hadn't wanted to hear his non committal words. Well practised, she imagined, from dismissing any other women who'd even hinted at getting too close.

But not hearing it hadn't made it hurt any less.

So where did that leave her? A night of hot, sweaty sex to fill the void left by the myth of her previous life and she was left feeling even worse than before.

Brilliant.

Although it probably was for the best. One night and she ached inside. How would she be in a week? Two weeks? Right now she barely knew him and she felt something. Could feel her traitorous romantic self lying in wait to fall for him. Because she didn't think it would take much at all to fall in love with Dan Halliday.

She pulled herself together, shoved her hand in her bag to find the familiar sharp folded edges of *The Sophie Project*. As always, it soothed her. She might have royally stuffed up the boyfriend part of the plan, but it would be okay. The wedding would be awful, but she'd survive—and she'd still have the rest of her plan. The rest of her new life to plot and schedule, and tick off neatly as required.

Who knew? Maybe a miracle would happen and she'd get *this* job. Maybe they wouldn't see massive oversleeping as a flaw in the prospective manager of their multimillion-dollar projects. Maybe.

She walked to the lift, the slap of her sandals an embarrassing echo in a marble tiled hallway more accustomed to stiletto heels. In the lift she hugged herself, watching the glowing floor numbers tick slowly downwards.

As the doors slid open she fished in her handbag for her phone, in readiness to call a taxi. Her head was down as she scrolled through her phone numbers for a taxi service when she heard a deep voice say her name.

She looked up, knowing it was Dan but not quite believing it until she saw him—propped against one of the pillars that dotted the skyscraper's foyer.

Shouldn't he be running for the hills?

He straightened his long body, walking towards her with steely intent.

'I didn't get to answer your question before. About the guidelines.'

She raised an eyebrow. 'I think you did.'

His gaze flicked away for a second, then back. 'No.' A pause. 'I didn't. Can we go somewhere quiet to talk?'

'This is fine,' she said, having no interest in delaying or extending this conversation in any way. She crossed her arms, waiting for him to continue.

'Look, Sophie, I like you...'

The words were as awkward as fingernails on a blackboard. Here it came. Surely there'd been no need for him to hang around? She'd already got it. Loud and clear.

It was fun, but I'm just not looking for a relationship.

Ugh. She couldn't bear it. 'Dan,' she said. 'Really, you don't have to bother. You're freaked out that I want something more from you, but I don't. I knew exactly what I was getting into. Sex. And that's it. I was hoping to keep the fun going a bit longer—you know, until the wedding—but if you'd rather not...'

What was she doing? Why prolong the inevitable? Did she really believe that she could do it—have a fling with Dan and not have it hurt like hell at the end?

He was looking at her with wide eyes that searched her

face. 'You just want something short-term? That's it? Nothing more?'

She snorted. 'Geez, Dan, you really *do* have tickets on yourself, don't you? I think you're right—what you said the other week. Maybe a fling is just what I need. I'm not ready for another relationship. Not yet.'

He blinked, but she knew she'd convinced him. She thought she might have half convinced herself.

Three weeks. With Dan. How many nights was that? Twenty-one? Mmm.

And she'd still get her wedding date. *The Boyfriend Plan* would remain on track.

All she had to do was remember why she'd kissed him under the tree outside Emma's. This was *only* about the want, about the electric chemistry between them and—how could she have forgotten this?—about the fact she didn't have to reveal the real emptiness inside her. Not to him, when it was only a fling.

If she'd just remember that, really—what could go wrong?

CHAPTER ELEVEN

THE first night of their fling Dan had taken her to dinner. To—in his words—'the best little Indonesian restaurant' in Northbridge, where the chairs were plastic, the floor faded vinyl and the lighting fluorescent.

It had been great, the food delicious and their casual conversation barely hiding the electricity that snapped between them. Following an impromptu—*ahem*—enthusiastic kiss outside a darkened shopfront before they'd even made it back to the car, the short drive back to Dan's had seemed impossibly long...but so definitely worth it.

The second night they'd had a fancy dinner—at Dan's place. Fully catered for by his chefs. Dan had tried—and failed—to convince her that his culinary skills went beyond his ability to reheat cannelloni in the oven. Although she wasn't going to complain about his creative uses for the strawberries and cream they'd had for dessert...

By the third night, when he picked her up from her mother's once again without giving her any warning about where they were going or what they were doing, Sophie decided he'd proved his point.

'Are you ever going to let me know your plans? Or is this going to be over two weeks of surprises?'

He glanced at her across the centre console before refocussing on the road. 'When it's so much fun watching you trying to figure things out? What do you think?'

She grinned. It was the strangest thing, but she was kind of *enjoying* having absolutely no idea what her plans were each evening. It was unexpectedly liberating to be unable to prepare or over-think what they were doing.

The lack of planning fitted perfectly with the whole fling, really—its very existence, of course, being completely unplanned. And also probably illogical. And not very sensible.

It was the first unwise decision she'd made so consciously—given her decision to waste years of her life with Rick had not seemed so unwise at the time. And so far it was fantastic.

Not that she'd thrown out *The Sophie Project*—not even close!—but Dan was like a drug: her daily dose of disorganisation amongst the regimentation of her charts and checklists.

On night three, Dan really had cooked for her—to prove his point—but by night four it was definitely her turn to be in charge.

By unspoken agreement they never confirmed their plans—or lack thereof—until late afternoon each day. They also never discussed when they would see each other next, which gave each night together a sense of impermanence that somehow heightened the intensity of each meeting.

Or maybe that was just how things were between them?

Sophie wouldn't let herself consider that point in too much detail.

So on night four she had Dan drive them to the same beach where they'd first kissed, stopping for a paper-wrapped package of fish and chips on the way. On the beach, they arranged themselves on colourful towels as they watched the sun set—with the thick cloud of tension that had hung between them at this same beach a few weeks earlier now replaced with humming anticipation.

Sophie studied him as he looked out to the still-glowing horizon, a lone seagull eating the remainder of his salted and vinegared chips beside him. They'd talked all evening—about the bar, about her old job in Sydney, anything, really. But it was nice, this comfortable silence. It felt so easy to just *be* with Dan.

The trill of his mobile phone made her jump and disturbed the bird. It retreated with a squawk and a few angry flaps of its wings.

Dan checked the caller ID and answered with an apologetic nod in her direction.

'Hi, Mum!' he said, and he leisurely rose to his feet, walking a few metres away, his bare feet sinking into the deep sand.

Sophie curled her own toes, hugging her knees to her chest. She hadn't really known what to expect with their fling—but whatever it was it had *not* been this. This was like all the best bits of a new relationship without any of the uncertainty or unnecessary complications. Knowing they had a deadline left her greedy to spend time with Dan without the fear of looking too keen or too desperate or any of the other myriad of angsty things that she usually tended to worry about.

Dan walked back towards her, his phone in his pocket. He reached out for her, pulling her to her feet. 'Ready to go?' he asked.

She'd been so busy watching him that she'd barely noticed how dark it had become.

'Yeah,' she said, pressing a quick kiss to his mouth.

They packed up quickly and headed towards the car.

'I won't be able to see you tomorrow,' Dan said as he unlocked the doors.

Sophie feigned nonchalance, determined not to ask why and to ignore the little kick of disappointment in her belly.

'Family dinner,' he said. 'My mum was just calling to ask what I wanted her to make.'

'That's nice,' she said, more relieved than she should be that he'd told her. Why? Was it really any of her business where he was when they weren't together?

Of course not.

'What are you having?' she asked, to distract herself as they climbed into the car. Hadn't she just decided that this fling was fabulous and completely free of uncertainty? And here she was, over-thinking.

Why couldn't she just let herself enjoy it for what it was?

Dan launched into an enthusiastic summary of the menu for the following evening as they drove back towards his house, describing the traditional Croatian dishes: *Pasticada*—marinated beef with gnocchi—and *blitva*—spinach with loads of potato, garlic and salt.

'That sounds amazing,' she said.

Dan grinned. 'It is. My mum would love to cook for you. I should take you one—'

The casually spoken words came to an abrupt halt and an awkward silence descended.

Sophie's mouth opened and closed a few times—but, really, what could she say? So she spent long minutes focussing on popping the naive little bubbles of hope that had formed, completely unwanted, inside her.

She knew Dan hadn't meant to say that. He didn't mean it.

Eventually they made it back to Dan's, and Sophie slid from her seat with no idea what to do. Should she call a taxi—go home? Dan had as good as built a wall between them, adding to it brick by brick with every passing second.

'Look, Dan, how about I—?'

But then he was beside her, crowding her against the car in the best possible way.

'Sophie,' he said with a hoarse whisper, and when his lips touched her she knew what he was doing. Erasing what he'd said and re-establishing exactly what they had.

Something hot and heavy and amazing…

And temporary. Definitely temporary.

Dan woke up before Sophie, as he had every morning that week, before even the earliest dawn light had forced its way through his window. He wasn't about to repeat the mistakes of that first morning they'd spent together—so he was already up early to swim before spending the rest of the day at one of his bars.

But, as always, he found himself dawdling. Letting his eyes adjust to the darkness so that he could watch Sophie sleep in the moonlight. It had been four of these mornings now, and she'd still never stirred as he watched her, tracing the curves and valleys of her body with his gaze.

If it bothered her, his early-morning disappearing act, she hadn't said a word.

And that surprised him. He hadn't believed her—not really—when she'd told him that all she wanted from him was a no-strings-attached fling. He hadn't forgotten the way she'd looked at him in his car the morning of her job interview, let alone that first time they'd made love. Her vulnerability, her depth of feeling, had been there for all to see—terrifying enough for him to know he had to end it after only one night.

But he hadn't been able to do it. He'd let himself believe what he was so sure was a lie so he could have what he wanted. Sophie.

For three weeks. Well, only two and a bit, now.

It seemed he'd been wrong. Sophie hadn't shown the slightest hint of wanting any more than he was prepared to give. Instead it was *him* saying stupid, silly things. Where had the almost invitation to meet his parents come from? It had been ten years since he'd last taken a woman to meet his family, and he had no intention—*absolutely none*—of changing that.

And yet the words had still slipped out. For a few seconds he'd imagined Sophie sitting beside him at his mum's funny 'statement piece' table: chatting, eating, laughing with his family.

He needed to make sure that didn't happen again. He *didn't* want that—not with Sophie, not with anyone.

He was lucky Sophie hadn't mentioned it—had seemingly forgotten the words had ever been said. Which was good—excellent, even. She understood exactly what their fling was: a bit of fun with a concrete, immovable end date.

So, with one last, long look at the beautiful woman sprawled beside him, he hauled himself out of bed and far away from her.

When Sophie woke, she knew she'd be alone. But even so, she found herself rolling over, reaching out with her hand, checking just in case…

But *no*. The sheets were empty and had long gone cold.

The first morning he'd left a note, but after that, nothing.

She told herself it didn't bother her, and that she really did need to adjust to this whole no-strings-attached thing, but still it stung. Just a little.

Especially when she compared it to that first morning, and how it had felt to fall asleep in his arms.

There had been no repeat of that, and she wasn't complaining—not really. It was her decision just as much as his—for, no matter how intimate, how intense it felt when she and Dan made love, they needed to maintain their boundaries.

Otherwise it would be all too easy to read more into their relationship. To think they even *had* a relationship, actually.

She knew that. He knew that.

It was sensible. It made things easier.

But still it stung.

After a quick shower, she headed home. It was still terribly early, but that was unavoidable. Test-driving cars might need to be shuffled a bit higher on her project plan task list. Returning the little red hatchback before her mother started work—or catching public transport if her mum needed the car for the night or if Dan had picked her up—well, it didn't really fit with her perception of what a glamorous fling should be.

When she unlocked her front door and stepped inside to find her mum seated in the middle of the couch, cereal bowl in lap, obviously waiting for her, she immediately decided it was not her new car that needed to be reprioritised. No, it was finding a new place to live.

Awkward conversations the morning after—with your mother—*definitely* did not a glamorous fling make.

'Have a good night?' her mum asked.

'Uh-huh,' she said, and a memory of Dan's body pressed up hard against her as he'd kissed her voraciously against his car popped, desperately unwanted, into her head. She blushed.

Her mum raised an eyebrow. 'Are you sure this is a good idea, Sophie? So soon after Rick?'

She had to give her mother points for waiting days before *The Talk*. Although Sophie hadn't exactly missed her pointed looks of concern.

She shrugged. 'It's nothing serious, Mum, okay? I can handle it.'

'Nothing serious to him, maybe,' her mum replied softly, and Sophie stiffened.

'For either of us,' she said firmly.

'You spend every night with a man you aren't serious about?' her mum asked, scepticism lining her face.

'I'm not seeing him tonight,' she said, choosing to ignore the fact that if she'd had her way she would be seeing him, every night. And not just because of the sex, no matter what she told herself.

'Hmm.' Her mum swallowed a mouthful of cereal, chewing slowly while all the time holding Sophie's gaze.

Her mum didn't believe her for one moment. She was sure Sophie was falling for him, and was sure she was going to get hurt.

And it wasn't news to Sophie that she was probably right. She'd gone into this knowing she was perched on the edge of a precipice—millimetres away from certain disaster.

But whether or not she'd already toppled over— Did it really matter? Walking away from him now would be no easier than watching him walk away from her.

And he would—in two weeks' time.

So she might as well, as she'd said with such bravado, *have fun* until then.

She would deal with the consequences later.

CHAPTER TWELVE

MORE than a week later Dan sat in his office and stared at his computer screen with eyes that refused to focus. He could hear the familiar sounds of a kitchen hand completing the final tidy-up of the kitchen, and he'd already heard the door slam multiple times as his staff headed home for the night.

It was Saturday, so Sophie was out there somewhere. She'd insisted on working, no matter how many times he'd told her that as far as he was concerned their deal was off. He was going to the wedding as her *bona fide* date. Not *bona fide* boyfriend, of course, but close enough that there was no longer any need to barter her waitressing skills.

But she'd insisted. *We had a deal*, she'd said. And then she'd given him the most withering look when he'd suggested he pay her.

He'd barely seen her all night. With the new bartender he wasn't needed behind the bar, so he'd just kept his normal eye on things, but otherwise been stuck to his office. He'd sorted out boring administration stuff while he'd spent far too much time thinking about Sophie.

Surely he should have hit his Sophie quota by now?

It had been thirteen days—twelve nights—since they'd agreed to have their fling, and so far he hadn't come close to having enough of her. They hadn't planned it, but the pattern of those first few days had continued, and they'd spent nearly every night together. One night they'd go out to dinner—and be in bed before dessert. Another they'd intend to go out—but never make it through the door. And for the remainder they just stopped even bothering to try. They'd eat takeaway while sitting cross-legged on his floor and then make love—on the couch, on the bed, against the wall…

The office door swung open. Sophie was a split second behind it. 'Everyone's gone but the cleaner,' she said. 'Are you ready to go?'

He shook his head. 'Come here,' he said gruffly.

She grinned and walked towards him. The room was lit only by the lamp on his desk and the glow of his computer screen. Her dark clothing blended into the darkness when the door clicked shut behind her.

She leant down and pressed a chaste kiss to his lips, but the soft touch wasn't even close to enough. His body had been anticipating this moment for hours—his blood simmering impatiently through his veins. Now he had her, he wasn't about to wait any longer.

He wrapped an arm around her waist, pulling her onto his lap with enough purpose to swivel the big leather office chair violently. She laughed as she fell against him, her breath warm against his neck.

'Very smooth,' she said.

He shrugged. 'Always.'

She snorted. 'Right. Nothing says suave like eating Chinese noodles out of plastic containers.' That had been dinner last night. 'And there I'd been, imagining you romancing women with silver service dining and the ballet.'

'Would you rather we went to the ballet?'

God, he hoped not.

She shook her head. 'What we're doing has been working just fine for me.'

Having her on his lap, legs hooked over the arm of his chair, was working pretty fantastically for him, too.

He kissed her—properly this time—his hand sliding under the fabric of her shirt to roam over the smoothness of her back and waist, holding her close against him.

She kissed him back with passionate enthusiasm, her arms looping around his neck.

By now he should be used to this, but every time they kissed it was just a little bit different. Sometimes fun. Sometimes impossibly intense. Sometimes slow. Sometimes desperate.

Sophie squirmed against him as he trailed kisses down her neck, her pretty sighs rapidly unravelling his control. But this was supposed to be just a prelude. They weren't alone yet.

And then she went still. Laughed.

Not the reaction he'd been aiming for.

'I don't believe it,' she said.

'What?'

She nodded over his shoulder at the computer screen that was now behind him. 'Dan Halliday has a project plan. And…' She laughed again. 'Is that a *spreadsheet*?'

He spun the seat around so he was again facing the desk. Sophie rearranged herself on his lap and leant forward to study the documents on the screen.

'I run a business—of course I have plans. The bars don't run themselves.'

She turned to look at him, raising an eyebrow. 'This is a five-year plan. A very, *very* detailed one.'

'So what?'

'You aren't as wild and spontaneous as you'd like me to think, are you?' she said, her eyes sparkling.

Rather than replying, he stood, lifting and turning her so she sat on the edge of his solid hardwood desk. She gasped as he stepped between her legs, his hands firms on her hips.

The humour in her expression was instantly replaced with heat, and her tongue darted out to moisten her lips.

'That sounds like a challenge to me.'

Sophie remembered hearing vaguely, right at the back of her mind, the cleaner call out a goodbye. She probably should've been embarrassed that she'd completely forgotten about him the moment Dan had kissed her. What if he'd heard them through the thin walls?

But now she lay—on Dan's *desk*!—completely spent, her breathing gradually slowing and returning to normal, and not for one second did she regret what had just happened.

It had never been like this for her before. This constant, continuous need for another person. This urgency, this want. He made her feel like someone else and yet paradoxically completely and totally herself. She barely recognised this woman who could make love with such abandon. But she revelled in how good, how right it felt.

Belatedly she registered that, unlike every other time they'd made love, Dan was not holding her in his arms, or kissing her, or making her smile with cheeky little whispers in her ear. Instead he stood with his back to her, his shoulders rising as he took long shuddering breath after long shuddering breath.

'Dan?' she said, her voice a husky tenor she barely recognised.

He shook his head. 'No condom,' he said, as if he couldn't believe it.

'It's okay,' she said, without thinking.

He turned, his gaze taking her in, propped up on her elbows, her knees bent at the table edge, her feet swinging in an unconscious rhythm. She stilled them.

'What do you mean it's okay? You could be pregnant.'
No, she couldn't.

Finally reality crashed in on her—brutal and uncompromising. She sat up, slid off the desk, searching for her underwear. For the first time she noticed the papers, the pens and other casualties of their passion lying scattered all over the floor.

Dan had located his boxers, and as she watched he dragged on his jeans in a rough, angry movement.

'I've *never* been so careless… How could I—?'

He muttered to himself as he paced the room. It was as if she wasn't even there.

She spotted the scrap of hot pink lace and satin and stepped into her underwear, then tugged down her shirt and refastened her bra. It didn't make her feel any less exposed, or any less guilty.

It's not your fault. We both got carried away…

Maybe. But she was the one who could end Dan's unnecessary torment. She knew he must be beside himself—that this was nightmarish for Mr Anti-Commitment.

She stood in front of him, halting him mid-stride. He rubbed his temples, looked at the floor, looked at her, looked at the door.

It didn't take a psychic to know exactly what he was thinking. He wanted nothing more than to put as much space between them as possible.

'It'll be okay,' she said again.

Now his attention locked on hers. 'You can't know that. Not for sure.'

Yes, she could.

She opened her mouth. No words came out.

He sighed. 'I know—odds are everything's fine. But what if it isn't?' Then his eyes widened hopefully. 'Unless you're on the pill?'

She couldn't lie outright to him. She shook her head. 'No.'

They stared at each other for long, long moments. At any one of those moments she could have chosen to tell him.

Why couldn't she? What was the problem?

Of any man, surely Dan was the most likely to be okay about her infertility? She'd be out of his life in a week's time, so why would he even care?

Weeks ago, on their first date, she'd justified not telling him because he didn't need to know. That excuse had just become invalid.

So it had come down to the other reason—the *real* reason she'd never told him when she'd blurted out and shared so much else with him.

She didn't want him to know. She'd *never* wanted him to know.

She'd told herself that the beauty of this fling was that she wouldn't have to tell him. But she'd lied to herself and pretended it was just generic resistance to revealing something so personal. That it wasn't about Dan, in particular, it was about having a man want her without knowing how flawed she was.

But of *course* it was all about Dan. It had been all about Dan from the beginning.

It wasn't that she couldn't handle yet another man rejecting her for her infertility—she couldn't handle that man being Dan.

At some point she'd closed her eyes.

Dan's finger brushed across her cheek as he tucked a strand of hair behind her ear. Her eyes slid open as he ran his hand across the top of her head, flattening what she only then realised must be the birds' nest of her hair.

'You look like you've been ravished,' he said, but his attempt at lightening the atmosphere fell horribly flat.

So they stood there together, mirror images of each other's misery.

He, because he thought there was a chance she might be carrying his baby.

She, because she knew—one hundred percent, gut-wrenchingly guaranteed—that she was not.

When Amalie had left him, Dan had bought the bar without any real planning or due consideration or anything even vaguely resembling the way he—the old Dan—normally did anything. That had been exactly why he'd bought it, and it had been perfect in its incongruousness.

It had distracted him, and given him a base on which to build his new life. And now the bar—well, *bars* now—was like a symbol. Proof that he'd changed from the person he'd once been to who he was now. The bars soothed him.

So it made sense that he went to his bar on Sunday morning—the morning after his brain explosion—when he'd let his hormones, his lust, suffocate his common sense. He certainly couldn't stay at home, where memories of Sophie were everywhere, even though she'd been careful never to leave behind any of her possessions.

The moment he stepped into the bar he realised his idiocy. The bar was where they'd met, where Sophie worked, and where last night they'd had the most overwhelming, all-consuming sex of his life. Today the bar had absolutely no chance of being his refuge.

He had the disconcerting thought that maybe it never would again.

So he drove to his parents' place. It was somewhere he'd never taken Sophie—a space where he could pull himself together, iron things out in his mind, without having memories of Sophie confusing him.

'This is a nice surprise!' his mother said when she answered the door. Then she must have seen something in his expression, because she did her standard 'worried mother' thing—reaching out to squeeze his hand and saying, 'Honey, is everything okay?'

He hadn't thought it possible, but it was right about then that he started to feel even *more* stupid. What was wrong with him?

Why couldn't he be logical and rational about this? Sophie was probably right. The odds were in favour of her not being pregnant. He had friends who'd tried for months or years before their wives or girlfriends had finally conceived. Given that, what was with all this panic? Why his rush last night to get home—alone—and as far away from Sophie as possible?

Although last night it hadn't been just him doing the running. Sophie had looked every bit as stricken as he'd felt, and had retreated equally fast. He hadn't heard from her this morning—although that in itself was not unusual. Since their fling had started they'd only communicated at night.

He followed his mother inside and sat quietly at the kitchen bench as she fussed about, making him a cup of coffee. She plonked it down in front of him and perched on a stool to his left.

'Do you want to tell me what's wrong?'

'No,' he said. 'Nothing's wrong. I just thought I'd pop by.'

She slanted him a pointed look. 'Dan—do you really think I'm that stupid?'

'Am I really that transparent?'

She looked at him shrewdly. 'Not usually, no.'

Just today. Great.

'Is it to do with work?' she asked, after a few minutes had passed.

That was a relief, at least. He didn't have his problem tattooed across his face.

Which should be unsurprising, though, given he couldn't identify the problem himself.

Was he angry at himself for forgetting about protection?

Yes, definitely.

But if it was just that, then surely this was where his logical self should kick in, telling him there was no point overreacting? Chances were it would be fine, and he should just wait a few weeks until he knew for sure either way. And, if Sophie was pregnant, deal with it then.

All very sensible.

All things he did not want to discuss with his mother. But there was something else bothering him—something that sat just out of reach and he couldn't grab on to, certainly couldn't define.

'No, it's not work. But I don't want to talk about it. Or think about it.'

Fortunately his mum heard his unspoken plea: *Distract me*.

So she did—or tried to—launching into a monologue about the events of the past week since he'd last spoken to her. Who she'd caught up with for coffee, the name of the book her book club was reading, that sort of thing. His dad joined them later, following some highly unsubtle facial expressions and hand gestures from his mother. Then he heard all about his dad's case, its latest developments, a series of precedent cases he was investigating.

He nodded and smiled at all the right places, but although he was listening barely any of it sank in. His brain was just too packed full of thoughts of Sophie. It seemed no matter where he went memories of her followed him.

How she'd looked—her hair a tangled mess but still beautiful—as she'd slept beside him. She wasn't a neat sleeper—she generally had an arm thrown above her head and her legs arranged all askew. But he liked that—the contrast to the perfectly groomed, perfectly organised Sophie she was by day. And it suited her, that sleepy disarray. It matched her innate passion—something he never would have guessed she possessed until they'd kissed that first time. After that it had seemed crazy that he'd never noticed it before.

Because Sophie's passion was in everything she did. He'd been so wrong to think that her spreadsheets and project plans sucked her dry of all feeling. Instead they channelled her passion, her dogged determination to make the absolute most of her second chance at life. Maybe he didn't always agree with what she was doing, and maybe her actions raised his eyebrows—her memorisation of cocktail recipes and her plan to take him clothes shopping came to mind—but she was always moving forward, always being authentically herself.

He loved that about her.

Loved?

Something of what he was feeling—shock, for example—must have been evident, for his mum reached out and squeezed his hand again.

'I'm sorry, honey. This wasn't the right time to tell you.'

He took a moment for the words to sink in. He couldn't recall a word his mum or dad had said in the previous few minutes. Now they stared at him with obvious concern.

'Tell me what?'

His parents shared a long look.

'That Nina lost her baby a few days ago,' his mum said quietly.

He blinked. 'But I just spoke to her the other day, after you told me she was pregnant. She said everything was fine.'

Her mum nodded. 'Sometimes things go wrong. It's not fair.'

Dan swirled his half-drunk and barely tasted coffee round and round in its mug. He felt sick for his cousin, who'd chatted to him so excitedly on the phone. She'd been so happy, but now her baby was gone.

He knew how *that* felt.

He stood up and walked outside onto the wide expanse

of jarrah decking. His parents' perfectly manicured over-sized garden was glorious in the midday sun, and while he couldn't see them, he could hear magpies in the branches of the ancient gumtrees.

No one followed him, leaving him to sit, alone, at the top of the steps leading down to the lawn.

It had been so long since he'd let himself think about his loss. About the baby he'd wanted so desperately. He could still remember how he'd felt when Amalie had announced her pregnancy: total euphoria. So all-encompassing that he'd not even noticed his wife's lack of the same. Because somehow he'd made her pregnancy all about *him*—about what *he* wanted and when, and about silly things: his excitement about remodelling the spare room as a nursery, about teaching his son or daughter how to swim, about one day his child following in his already successful career footsteps.

All about Dan. Him, him, him.

He'd been so caught up in that—in *his* plans and dreams for the future—that he'd not spent any time in the present. So he hadn't seen what was happening right in front of his face.

And then it had been too late—far too late. His baby was gone. His wife had begun divorce proceedings.

So he'd changed his life. Become the opposite of the man he'd once been. Shoved aside his old hopes and dreams—at first because it had hurt too much and later because he'd decided it wasn't worth the risk of hurting like that again.

Or of hurting someone else like that again.

Was that it? Was that what had caused him to toss and turn all night? The niggling sensation that maybe his long-discarded dreams did not lie as dormant as he'd thought?

Because even once his initial knee-jerk, confirmed-bachelor, ultra-cautious reaction had finally blown over—and it had taken hours after Sophie had climbed into her car and

driven away—he'd not let himself consider—*really* consider—what he'd feel if Sophie *was* pregnant.

How would he feel? If Sophie was carrying his child?

Their child?

Scared. Anxious. That was to be expected.

But that wasn't all. Somewhere deep inside him, amongst
the fear and the hurt and the angst of ten years earlier, was
a tiny pinprick of hope.

Burning warm and bright.

CHAPTER THIRTEEN

The Sophie Project 2.1 (Project Manager: S. Morgan):
Sub Project: The Boyfriend Plan

S‍HE had to end it.

Soon. Immediately, really.

Sophie lay fully clothed on her bed—the same narrow bed she'd slept in as a child and as a teenager. She was now blessedly alone, as her mother had left for her Sunday evening rock 'n' roll dance class after a morning full of concerned motherly *Are you okay*?s and *Do you want to talk about it*?s. She was very grateful her mother hadn't rolled out any *I told you sos*. Although she definitely would've deserved them.

Was it really only two weeks since Emma's barbecue? Two weeks since she'd thrown herself into something so hot and so wonderful with Dan—and simultaneously so ill-advised and so stupid?

It seemed impossible.

Last night she'd driven home in floods of pathetic tears, juggling the bone-deep emotions that roller-coastered about inside her. On the surface she'd cried for that old ache, that old emptiness, its familiarity doing nothing to lessen the hurt. But beneath that the real pain lingered, and for once it had nothing at all to do with her infertility.

It was irrational, she knew, to be so devastated by Dan's

reaction. They were having a fling—a fling with such a clear end date that of *course* he would panic at the possibility of being tied to her for ever. She knew a pregnancy was impossible, but *he* didn't, and his fear had been etched all over his face.

What had she expected? Some romantic platitude? A promise that they would get through this together?

Ha! Ridiculous.

Right from the start she'd known what they had and all that Dan would ever offer her. She'd thought she'd recovered from her silly little slip-up on the first night, when she'd confused sex with intimacy and had thought she'd been handling her first attempt at a no-strings-attached fling with remarkable aplomb. She'd actually *believed* that!

And then they'd both forgotten about protection, and her first reaction had been sorrow that she would never have Dan's child.

Completely forgetting that Dan certainly didn't want children with her.

So she'd been kidding herself. She hadn't jumped into bed with Dan purely because he made her feel wanted and needed—although of course that had been part of it.

The main reason—the reason she'd been hiding from herself—was that she liked him.

Really, *really* liked him. Daydreaming-of-for-ever liked him.

Her inability to tell him the truth had made that clear. She didn't want him to know, because the last man she'd loved had rejected her for what she was incapable of giving him.

She just couldn't risk that happening again—not so soon.

And that, of course, was the terrible irony of all this. Dan didn't even know about her infertility and he *still* didn't want her. She was tying herself up in knots over telling him something that to him would be completely irrelevant.

She didn't even know if he *wanted* children! Their conversations had certainly never veered towards the future, but based on his general attitude towards relationships and marriage it didn't take much to connect the dots. It seemed as if she had found a guy who genuinely didn't want children…there was just the pesky little problem that he didn't want her, either.

She had got embarrassingly far ahead of herself. She'd actually let herself believe the intimacy they shared was more than physical! She'd totally forgotten—or, if she was honest, deliberately ignored—the fact that Dan was always going to walk away from her.

So delaying the inevitable was doing her no favours.

She needed to end it now.

Belatedly, Sophie realised that *love* had crept into her thoughts.

Did she love Dan?

She couldn't even bear to consider it.

A loud knock on the front door was like a thunderclap in the perfectly silent house. Sophie scurried to the door in her comfiest tracksuit pants and a faded singlet, hugely relieved she hadn't been crying. At least her mother's visitor wouldn't have to suffer *that* unfortunate, blotchy-faced vision.

She opened the door, speaking before it had fully swung open.

'Sorry, my mum isn't home at the—?'

The sentence died an abrupt death at the ghastly reality of who it was framed in the doorway.

'Can I come in?' Dan said.

So he was going to beat her to the chase, then? End it himself?

Unsurprisingly, it didn't make her feel any better.

She didn't say a word—just stepped aside to let him in. As he walked past she could smell the familiar scent of him—

crisp aftershave mixed with the ocean-fresh washing powder she'd seen in a box in his laundry.

They both stood awkwardly in the middle of her mother's lounge room, a slight breeze softly rattling the venetian blinds.

Sophie didn't know the appropriate etiquette in this situation. Did you offer a man a drink or a seat when he was visiting for the purpose of dumping you?

She decided *no*, and simply crossed her arms and stood there—waiting.

'Sophie,' he said. 'I'm sorry about last night. I over-reacted.'

She nodded. 'And?'

He looked confused. 'And...I'm *really* sorry.'

She met his gaze. 'Come on. I saw the way you freaked out last night. Isn't this where you say it's been fun, but maybe it's best we end it now?'

'Is that what you want me to say?'

'Yes,' she said. *No.*

His brow crinkled. 'Why?'

She shrugged, feigning nonchalance. 'This was never supposed to be anything serious, Dan. Don't you think last night cut a bit too close to the bone? We've only got a week to go—wouldn't it be easier to end it now?'

'You want to end this? End us?'

She laughed—a short burst of ugly sound. 'I thought you were very clear that there isn't an *us*. That there will never be an us.'

What was she doing? Why bother to explain?

Why couldn't she channel some ultra-sophisticated woman who effortlessly flitted from affair to affair?

He stepped towards her. 'What if I've changed my mind?'
What?

'But you don't do relationships.'

Another step closer.

'Maybe I'd like to make an exception.' He was watching her, his gaze steady and intense, his brilliant blue eyes piercing her soul. 'If that's okay with you?'

He meant it.

It was so unexpected, so startling, that constructing a sentence was suddenly completely beyond her. 'Oh.'

'Oh?' he said with a smile. But she saw the hint of vulnerability behind it.

Was this really happening?

'Why?' she said.

'I don't know,' he said, low and seductive. 'I think we fit pretty well together.'

He was close enough now that his breath fanned her cheek, and her fingers itched to reach out and touch him. All she had to do was give him the slightest signal and she'd be in his arms, his mouth on hers, his hands all over her body.

She took a deep breath, desperately trying to prevent herself from dissolving into a boneless puddle of want. His nearness never failed to accelerate her pulse and heat her skin, and it would be easy—so, so easy—to just...

No. This was too important. She *needed* to understand.

'What else? Surely I'm not the only woman you've been sexually compatible with?'

The stark words were intended to strip all hint of romance from what they'd shared together, and they were effective—to a point. Dan took a step backwards.

'What's going on here, Soph? There's more than something physical happening between us—or am I imagining things?'

Again she was trapped by an inability to lie to him. She shook her head.

'Then why? I thought this was what you wanted?'

'But it's what you *don't* want. So what's changed, Dan?

Why does a confirmed bachelor suddenly want a relationship? And what makes him change his mind overnight?' She took a deep breath, locking her gaze with his. It didn't make any sense, but she needed to be sure. 'The only thing I can see that's changed is now you think I could be pregnant.'

'You could be.'

'I'm *not*,' she said, her voice immovably firm.

He moved closer to her again, this time reaching out for her, rubbing his hand along her upper arm. Her skin goosepimpled at his touch.

'That is what's changed,' he finally conceded, and her whole body tensed in response. 'I've avoided relationships since my divorce because I was so scared of repeating past mistakes. But you—' he smiled as his gaze explored her face '—you've reminded me of what I'm missing out on. That's sometimes it's worth the risk of making a mistake.'

His words should be making her glow with happiness. He thought she was special. Maybe even thought he could fall for her.

But she needed to know the truth.

'What happened? Between you and your wife?'

Now it was his turn to tense. She saw him put the familiar shutters and 'Keep Out' signs in place. She'd seen them often enough.

But then he shook his head, and all the barriers fell away.

'I told you, didn't I, that I once had my own life plan?' She nodded. 'It was a good one. Degree, fiancée, great job, nice house, marriage, pay rises…babies.'

Sophie sucked in a harsh breath.

'I had this image in my head—like a painting of what success was supposed to be. I don't know where I got it from, but I was obsessed with it—and obsessed with achieving it as quickly as possible. I didn't see the point of waiting around. I wanted *everything*, and I wanted it *now*.' He shrugged, but looked anything but casual. 'And as I'd got everything else in my life whenever I wanted it, I had no reason to think I wouldn't.'

'So you became a lawyer, got married…'

'And Amalie got pregnant.'

Oh, God. Oh, God. Oh, God…

She couldn't look at him, so she looked at the floor as her limbs went heavy with dread.

'I was so excited. It was what I'd always wanted, you know?'

Sophie nodded—a stiff jerking action. Was this really happening? *Dan* wanted kids? She looked up as he ran his hands through his hair violently—an angry, furious movement.

'I'd just forgotten to make sure it was what Amalie wanted too. She was younger than me—a couple of years. It never occurred to me that she didn't want a baby as badly as I did. I barely registered her lack of enthusiasm; I was so caught up in my own.'

Dragging her eyes away from him seemed impossible now. Every line on his face was taut with decade-old torment. She reached for him, grabbing his hand.

'But Amalie couldn't handle it. I came home from work one day to find her sitting at the kitchen table. She told me she was leaving me, that she'd made a mistake—she wasn't ready for marriage and kids and happy families.' He paused, took a deep breath. 'She said she wanted her youth back.'

More than anything Sophie wanted to turn back time and rewrite their whole conversation. Why did she have to ask? Why did she have to push? Why was she putting Dan through this agony?

But it was like a hurtling boulder now—impossible to stop.

'Amalie…she…' Another deep breath. This one a little shaky. That weakness was shocking in such a strong man. 'She'd aborted our baby.'

It was as if she could feel his pain, shooting from some-where inside him and flowing from where their hands joined. Her heart shattered for his loss.

'Oh, Dan…' she said, any other words she could think of manifestly inadequate. She wanted to throw her arms around him, somehow absorb his emotions and dilute his hurt. But she could do nothing but stand there, the horrible knowl-edge of where this conversation was headed freezing her to the spot.

He shook his head. 'I've never told anyone that. No one even knew she was pregnant but us.'

'You blame yourself,' she said. A statement.

'She felt trapped. She said it was the only way out.' His gaze flicked away, over her shoulder to the quiet suburban street through the window. 'I was so focused on work and what I wanted I wasn't paying attention. I wasn't listening.'

'But you were married. I assume you'd discussed having children?' He nodded. 'But she changed her mind?'

'Yes.'

Frustrated anger bubbled inside her for what Dan had had ripped away from him.

'Abortion wasn't her only option. That was her choice and not your fault.'

He shook his head again, dismissing her words. 'I screwed up my marriage.'

'And that's why you avoid relationships?'

'Until now,' he said, his gaze reconnecting with hers. 'I *am* a different person to who I was then, and besides, I know you'll never let me take over your life.' He grinned, but she didn't return his smile. 'When I thought about it, when I got past all my default panicking and over-reacting last night, I imagined how I'd feel if you *were* pregnant. And I realised I didn't feel like I'd expected. I know it wouldn't be what we'd planned, and it'd be far from ideal, but—well, it made me feel kind of good. Like I'd been given a second chance.'

Sophie's gut churned. Her throat tightened inexorably.

'And if you're not pregnant, then... Well—I'd like to just see what happens. Maybe one day...'

The hopeful sparkle in her eyes triggered an icy wave of nausea. How was this possibly fair? How was it fair that she'd met this man who wanted her—wanted a future with her—but also wanted children? How could this have happened again?

'I'm not pregnant, Dan.'

He looked bemused. 'I know it's probably unlikely, and that all this must be a bit of a surprise. I mean, it's a pretty big surprise for me, too—'

'Dan. *Stop.* I need you to listen to me.'

Finally he seemed to register that she wasn't reacting normally.

He squeezed the hand he still held. 'Did I read this wrong? You're *not* interested in anything longer term?'

'You didn't read me wrong.'

His broad smile would have been beautiful if she'd been any other woman.

She held his gaze as she struggled to find the courage to speak again. As the silence lengthened Dan's smile gradually fell away.

'Dan, I *know* I'm not pregnant. It's impossible.' She had to force her lips to move, blinking away the beginnings of fat, ugly tears. 'I can't have children.' A shuddering breath, but she had to make sure he understood. 'I'm infertile.'

Silence.

She was sure time stood still as the all-consuming nothingness enveloped them. She couldn't hear a thing—not even the sound of her own breathing.

Stupidly, she'd hoped she'd somehow got it wrong. That by

a second chance he'd meant a future with her—alone. That another child was not intrinsic to his rediscovered hopes and dreams.

His gaze didn't shift from hers, but it changed. She saw it. The moment that sparkle, that hopeful, excited flicker, faded before her eyes.

And finally disappeared.

No, she hadn't got it wrong.

He dropped her hand and it fell, heavy and useless, against her thigh. *Then* the silence lifted—only to be replaced with the roaring in her ears.

She staggered away from him—away from his sudden coldness. From his unvoiced but oh, so obvious rejection.

The backs of her knees hit the couch and she fell awkwardly, her hip smacking its arm before she landed in its enveloping softness. She welcomed the pain, the reminder that she was alive when she felt as if part of her was dying.

Too late, he spoke.

'Sophie, I'm so sorry…'

Dan didn't know what to do. Certainly not what to say.

His words trailed off, useless and without meaning.

Sophie sat exactly as she'd landed on the couch, awkwardly and uncomfortably, her gaze trained on nothing through the wide lounge room window.

He felt pole-axed. Unloading his ten-year secret had lifted a weight he'd had no idea he was carrying. Nothing would erase his loss, or his guilt, but telling Sophie—having her know—it had helped. He hadn't planned it, but it had felt right.

And then…

She'd told him. And he'd been sure he felt something break deep inside.

'Have you figured it out yet?' she asked, her eyes shining with unshed tears but still not looking in his direction.

'Figured what out?'

'The real reason Rick dumped me. Isn't it obvious?'

He went to her, planning to sit beside her, but now she met his gaze and shook her head. A sharp, clear directive: *Stay away.*

'Didn't he know?' He had a thought. 'Did *you* know?'

She choked out a bitter laugh. 'He knew. I've always known—it was the cancer. For ever ago.'

'But he changed his mind?'

'Yeah. Funny thing, that. Men wanting to get married and have children. Who would have thought it?'

He let the dig deflect off him as he remembered something she'd told him that first night. Rick's new girlfriend was already pregnant.

Dan ached for Sophie, and without thinking he reached for her.

'Don't.'

They fell into another infinite silence.

'You don't have to stay,' she said finally.

'I don't want to go,' he said. And he didn't. He wanted nothing more than to drag her into his arms and do *something* to obliterate the misery that cloaked her.

'But what would be the point, Dan? Aren't we right back where we started? Short-term material only?'

'No…' But even as he spoke he was blindsided by the truth of her words.

Her infertility changed everything. His time with Sophie had shown him what he wanted—had shown him what he was missing out on. He was older, wiser, but the core of his old dream remained.

And he wanted the whole deal—he wanted marriage. He wanted kids. He *needed* to rewrite his past—to correct his past mistakes. To heal his ancient pain.

'Who would have thought it?' she said, her tone high

pitched and false. 'Dan Halliday, the ultimate bachelor, wants to settle down and have kids!'

'That is what I want,' he said, regret weighing down his words. 'I'm sorry, Sophie.' As if that was even close to enough.

She surged to her feet, a whirlwind of jagged emotions. She slammed into him and his arms embraced her naturally, hers wrapping untidily behind his neck.

And then she kissed him—a kiss that tasted like salty tears and passion and want and need and...love?

He kissed her back, powerless to do anything but caught up in her desperation and realising that it was also his. Burning, swirling, edgy desperation that felt as if it would go on for ever—and then ended far too soon.

They broke apart, panting.

'Is that enough for you?' she asked. 'Can *I* be enough for you? Just me?'

She stood before him, her expression raw and revealing.

With every awful passing second he sensed her slipping away from him. But he was helpless—completely helpless to stop it.

Suddenly she straightened her shoulders and walked with stiff-legged determination to the front door. She wrenched it open, her face perfectly expressionless and unmoving.

'I love you, Dan,' she said, as if it was a curse. 'But it's time for you to go.'

CHAPTER FOURTEEN

The All New Sophie Project
(Project Manager: S. Morgan)

SOPHIE hung up her phone with some satisfaction as she walked briskly down the city street. Her new plan was already off to a fantastic start. She'd just been offered a job—from the purple-painted toenails interview, no less. She had high hopes for this plan—primarily because it had absolutely no reference to men, or boyfriends, or wedding dates, or anything even vaguely related to the opposite sex.

And that was A Very Good Thing.

This time her plan was truly just about *her*. Now, finally, she'd be able to get her life on track.

She arrived—early, of course—at the café where she was meeting Emma for lunch, so had a few minutes to fish her ubiquitous project plan out of her handbag and spread it out carefully on the table.

Using a new red felt-tip pen, bought specifically for the purpose, she crossed out *'Get a fabulous job that you will love!'* She'd decided to think positive with this plan. It was tempting to cross out *'Buy totally impractical yet super-sexy car',* but she did still need to confirm the finance on the lipstick-red hard-top convertible she'd test-driven that morning. With that in mind, she phoned her bank.

Emma arrived just as she ended the call, and she scribbled out the car task with much enthusiasm as Emma slid into her seat.

'Ah, Sophie and her project plans!' Emma said, smiling. 'I remember these from school. You're the only person I know who project-managed her Year 12 group assignments. What's this one for? Buying a house? A holiday?'

'My life,' she said simply.

Emma barely raised her eyebrows. 'Really? How does that work?'

Sophie spent a few minutes running her through the project.

Emma nodded. 'So where does the delicious Dan fit in with all of this?'

She quickly folded up the project plan and shoved it in her handbag. 'He doesn't.'

'No?' Emma said.

'Yes,' she said dryly. 'As of a few days ago.' Sophie was impressed by how nonchalant she sounded—not as if she could rattle off, almost to the minute, how long it had been since Dan had walked out through her front door.

'What happened?'

'We wanted different things,' she said. That was a significant understatement.

Emma nodded, but her old friend wasn't about to let her get off that easy. 'What kind of things?'

'Oh, the usual.' She shrugged. 'He wants children. I can't have them. You know.'

'Oh, Soph,' Emma said, dragging her chair around the table so she could wrap her arm round her.

And so the whole story came out—with a few selected omissions. The interlude up against Emma's jacaranda for one. More importantly the baby Dan had lost, for another.

But Emma got the gist of it, not even blinking when Sophie admitted to the lies she'd told her, and had planned to tell at Karen's wedding.

'We should have thought about how you'd feel, Sophie. I've never forgotten the indignity of being a single person at a wedding. After what happened with Rick, of *course* you considered it a nightmare.'

'Trust me—it's the least of my worries right now,' she said. 'I'm actually kind of looking forward to it.'

It would a blessed few hours' distraction from the blow-by-blow re-enactment of that last conversation with Dan that spun like a carousel around and around in her mind.

How had she managed to shut Rick out of her thoughts in the aftermath of their break-up? She'd tried her old techniques, her methods to keep her mind busy, but they'd all failed. It felt as if twenty-four hours a day all she could think of was Dan.

Dan. Dan. Dan.

It was awful.

Hadn't she read somewhere that the time it took to get over a break-up was approximately half the length of the actual relationship? With that formula she should have been over Dan in practically a matter of hours. Given she hadn't given Rick a second thought in weeks, and at the moment couldn't fathom forgetting about Dan, she decided that theory had substantial flaws.

'I can't believe he said that,' Emma said with a sad shake of her head. 'That he couldn't love just you. He seemed like such a nice guy.'

'Well,' she conceded, 'he didn't say that, exactly. I said that. He just didn't disagree.'

Emma's eyes lit up. 'So he *doesn't* believe that?'

'Yes, he does,' Sophie said, remembering his expression with too much clarity. There was no doubt in her mind as to what he thought. Just like Rick, Dan needed her to come as some package deal. He wasn't interested in faulty goods.

'Has he been calling you?' Emma asked, surprising her.

'Yes,' she said. 'But I haven't answered.'

'Uh-huh. So how do you know for sure?'

'I just *know.*'

Emma snorted. 'Why? Because it all went according to your plan?'

Sophie jerked away from Emma's no longer comforting arm. 'What are you talking about? I didn't *plan* the break-up.'

'Maybe not, but had you already decided what was going to happen? Maybe you convinced yourself that his rejection was inevitable?'

Sophie bristled. 'Emma, if there'd been any hint of another outcome I would have grabbed it. I'm in love with him.'

'Oh, Soph,' Emma said, pulling her close again. 'Maybe this is my delusionally romantic, happily married self talking, but I saw something special between you two. Do me a favour—next time he calls, answer. Just so you're sure.'

Reluctantly, and two strong coffees later, Sophie agreed.

But Dan didn't call her again.

Dan had tried calling her for three days. Not crazy, stalker-type phone calls—just a single phone call each day. Asking her how she was. Asking her if she'd talk to him.

But she'd never responded, and eventually he'd decided he was just being pathetic.

It was over. What was the point?

He didn't really even know what he wanted to talk to her about. To apologise for his less than well-handled reaction? Definitely. But what else?

It wasn't as if he could make it all better with a *Whoops! Changed my mind. I actually don't want to have children.* Because that wouldn't be true.

To be brutally honest, he didn't have a clue what he wanted to say to her. He just knew he wanted to see her again. He wanted to somehow make everything magically right.

But of course he knew that was impossible.

On the day of the wedding he went to his parents' place for lunch. At home, he'd tried his best to pretend it was just a normal Saturday, and that absolutely nothing special or unusual or of any concern was happening that day.

He'd failed, dismally, so had headed for Peppermint Grove, shoving all thoughts of Sophie alone at the wedding she'd so dreaded out of his mind. Or at least trying really, *really* hard to do that.

Much to his frustration, he was no more successful once he arrived, but he did his best to pay attention to the conversation.

His legs jiggled as his parents spoke, his toes tapping on the polished wooden floor. He had absolutely no idea what they were saying. None.

This time he couldn't even nod or smile at the appropriate places. They could easily have been speaking in another language. Or gobbledegook. Or discussing their plans to join a cult in Far North Queensland. He heard absolutely nothing.

Eventually even his long-suffering parents got sick of him.

His father reached out and took his untouched plate away. 'Is there somewhere more important you need to be, Dan?'

That sentence sank in, hitting him like a lightning bolt and shuffling his convoluted thoughts into something clean and simple and straightforward.

Yes, he did need to be somewhere. He needed to go to the wedding.

He might not be able to offer her anything more, but he *could* hold up his end of their deal. Help her cross something else off her project plan.

One wedding date.

On his way.

Thanks to the carefully photocopied invitation stored neatly in the back of his own project file—complete with handy map—Dan had absolutely no problem getting himself to the wedding venue. He was even on time—well, close enough.

He turned down the long red bitumen driveway of a winery, cutting between perfectly parallel rows of vines to park outside the timber and iron reception centre, its wide verandahs promising spectacular views of the Swan Valley.

But he paid little attention to the scenery as he followed the hand-painted signs to the ceremony. He crested a hill to find the wedding spread out beneath him: a white narrow carpet leading to a rose-entwined gazebo, guests fanned out in a near perfect semi-circle, the metallic ribbon of the river an undulating, glistening backdrop.

There were a *lot* of guests—so many that it took him several minutes before he found Sophie. But there she was, right in the thick of it beside the aisle, the silver glint of her purse reflecting the glare of the sun.

It was just as he joined the very fringes of the crowd that it occurred to him that maybe this wasn't his best idea.

Around him couples stood, hand in hand or arm in arm, some talking, some looking perfectly content to just be in each other's company. A mother squatted down to her child's eye-level to explain how important it was to stay perfectly quiet during the wedding; her daughter nodded solemnly in reply. An older woman with gleaming white hair twisted awkwardly in one of the few seats, her expression vivid with joyful anticipation of the bride's impending arrival.

Around him everywhere was love.

If he'd been able to accept Sophie's love he'd be right beside her now. His arm around her, the supple press of her body against him.

He'd deserve to be here then.

Now he was the last person she'd want to see. He was—far too late—absolutely sure of that.

A man in front of him stepped aside, revealing Sophie only metres away.

She stood, her back to him, the straps of her dress displaying a perfect V of skin—skin that looked even more fragile and pale than usual against the dark silvery-grey fabric. Her hair was up, looped and pinned, and when she turned her head just slightly he could see a hint of her deep pink lips.

He wanted nothing more than to go to her, but knew he had no right. What had he really expected to happen? For Sophie to be *grateful* he'd come? For her to agree the past few days had never happened and go back to how it was before?

There was about as much chance of either of those things happening as of him returning to a career in law.

He realised that coming to the wedding had never been about Sophie. It was all about him. He'd needed to see her one more time.

But now he had to go.

He turned just as every other person in the vicinity did exactly the same thing. The bride had arrived.

With a quick getaway now impossible, he slid behind two tallish guests and hoped to hell Sophie hadn't seen him. He risked a glance at her. He was the only guest not watching the bride make her way towards the aisle.

He needn't have worried. Sophie's attention was one hundred percent focused on her old friend, a telltale sheen to her eyes. Happy tears—not the other kind that he was far too familiar with.

He didn't take his eyes off Sophie as the bride continued

her journey, his gaze greedy as he made the most of this last time he would see her.

And then, finally, the bride arrived beside her groom and the ceremony began.

At first Dan barely paid attention, but soon found himself caught up in the undeniable beauty and romance of the moment. The firm, respectful handshake between the father of the bride and the groom; an only slightly stumbling poetry reading from a young girl; the stolen private smiles between the couple who kept getting lost in each other's eyes.

'I, Ben, take you, Karen, to be my friend, my lover, my wife...'

It was a perfect moment. Picture-perfect, really—as the click and whirr of many cameras attested.

It was just like his moment with Amalie, all those years ago. They'd stood together just the same—although in a church rather than under the afternoon sun. He'd thought he'd loved her so much then, and had dreamed of their picture-perfect future: their home together, their future children...

Now Karen was saying her vows. 'I promise to be there when you need me, to comfort you and encourage you, to be your best friend everlasting...'

They were so different from his more traditional vows. These were all about togetherness, support. Friendship.

Had Amalie ever been his best friend?

He knew the answer to that. He'd been so caught up in achieving his goal—striving for some mythical watercolour-painted perfection—that he'd never stopped to just *be*. To be with his wife. To be together as a couple just for who they were and not for what they could achieve together. Not for what life goals she could help him tick off his list.

That mistake had cost him his marriage and his child.

Sophie had made him realise that he *was* ready to try again. To do it right this time and not repeat his old mistakes.

Something—the sparkle of sunlight against her hair, or

maybe just that constant magnetic pull between them—drew his gaze to Sophie as she turned, her darkest blue eyes capturing his with shock. Then joy—for a fleeting second—before transforming to distress in an instant.

Suddenly the truth was obvious. Painfully, embarrassingly, wonderfully so.

He loved Sophie.

And if he didn't do something quickly he *was* going to make the same mistakes. Hell, he'd already made one hugely massive one—walking away from Sophie because she could never have his children.

Was it really children he desperately wanted? Or the chance to rewrite history? And what had driven him to tell Sophie his darkest secret? The possibility that she was carrying his child? Or the reality that he had fallen in love with her?

He could never replace the child he'd lost, just as he could never have a 'do-over'—even if Sophie *could* have children. To think he could only diminished the memory of his child, and reduced what he'd had with Sophie to little more than cardboard characters following a decade-old script.

Sophie deserved more than that. *He* deserved more than that. He was a different person. He'd grown, he'd changed—and so had his dreams. This was his chance to re-start his life after years of punishing himself.

He had been partly right. This *was* his second chance—but just not the way he'd thought. He'd always ache for the baby he'd never got to meet, and he felt a pang of sadness that with Sophie he would never have children—but that pain was incomparable to the agony of losing her.

In a perfect world, yes, he would want children with Sophie. But that was the key thing: *with Sophie*. Without her, what would be the point?

By pushing Sophie away he was robbing himself of a chance at happiness—and all for some stupid picture in his head.

It was time for a new picture—a picture of just him and Sophie, together. Laughing, living…loving.

And he realised with bone-deep certainty that *nothing* was missing from that picture. With Sophie he'd have everything he needed.

This time the picture was all about love.

If she'd ever forgive him.

The sudden wave of applause jolted Sophie out of the grip of Dan's relentless gaze. She turned to witness the final seconds of Karen and Ben's kiss, trying as hard as she could to focus on them and not on Dan's unexpected appearance.

What was he doing here?

She could feel his eyes still on her, but she kept her body rigidly turned away as the bridal party made their way back down the aisle and away for their photos. She didn't look at him as the guests drifted back up the hill to the champagne and canapés that awaited them.

When they were finally alone, she did turn to face him. She'd known he hadn't left—had felt his presence so assuredly she'd had no doubt he hadn't moved.

She crossed her arms, flicking her gaze up and down his length. He wore a charcoal suit and a pale green tie—the perfect coincidental match to her silver-and-grey outfit. They would've looked great together…

'Why are you here?' she asked, forcing herself back into the present and out of dreams of what could've been. So what if they'd look good together? She should know by now not to judge based on the superficial. Dan was certainly far from what he'd seemed.

'I thought I'd be your wedding date—'

'I'm doing just fine, thank you,' she said, her words brisk and crisp. 'Your services are no longer required.'

He nodded. 'I know. It was obvious the moment I saw you.'

She shifted her gaze, focusing on the knot of his tie. 'Then why are you still here?'

He walked a few paces towards her, but she walked backwards an equal distance, not willing to close the gap between them.

'Watching that ceremony, I realised I made a mistake. Sophie, I—'

She snorted. 'Don't tell me *you* got caught up in the romance? Mr Anti-wedding?' She let her gaze creep upwards, meeting his. 'I don't want to hear some soppy declaration that will wear off before Karen's honeymoon's over. I *heard* what you said on Sunday, Dan. I know what's important to you. I can't give you what you want—simple. A relationship between us is a waste of time.'

There. The pointlessness of them perfectly encapsulated.

If only she could dismiss the still-raw, pulsing emotions inside her so easily.

But he didn't seem to be listening. He strode towards her and too late she realised she'd backed herself up against the gazebo. She was planning to dart around him and away— far away—when she saw the look in his eyes. They were intensely blue. Electric. A shade she'd never seen before.

So, despite her better judgement, she stayed.

'You know what, Sophie? Bad luck. You are *getting* a soppy declaration—like it or not.'

Her stupid bruised heart leapt, refusing to listen to her sensible self. Nothing that Dan would say could possibly fix things.

'I feel like I've been stumbling around in the dark for ten years,' he said. 'Convinced that by becoming the opposite of myself things would be okay.'

'But now you realise that you aren't really the person you thought you'd become,' she interrupted, her voice heavy. 'That you still want the same things—a wife, children.'

'No,' he said. 'That's where I got it wrong. I mixed up how I felt for you with the old Dan from before. I made the mistake of thinking about where that feeling could take me, not appreciating and experiencing it for what it was. Sophie, you've transformed what was once dark inside me to light. I can't comprehend not having you in my life.'

She wouldn't let the words sink in—wouldn't let herself believe them. 'But you wanted a second chance at a family. I can't give you that.'

'No, Sophie. I *have* a second chance, period. I can't replace my child—no more than I can replace you. Being with you is what's most important to me. Just you.'

The words were beautiful, and so tempting.

'No,' she said firmly, shaking her head. 'You'll change your mind. One day you'll realise that your life isn't complete without children. That you want more than just me.'

Even if he *did* mean it today, she knew it would never, ever last. It would just be a matter of time, and she couldn't put herself through the awfulness of loving Dan while a clock ticked inescapably downwards.

'Is that what Rick told you?' he asked, his eyes so full of care and understanding that she ripped her gaze away. 'That he had to have children?'

'Yes,' she said tightly.

His expression shifted abruptly to the tense lines of anger. 'Did he say you weren't enough for him?'

She nodded, her gaze fixed on the ground. 'He said he *loved* me, but it wasn't enough.' A pause, and then nothing more than a whisper, *'I'm not enough.'*

He reached for her, but she turned away, his touch just a

brief brush against her arm. 'Sophie, you're all I want. All I need.'

'How can I ever trust that?' she said, sorrow mixed with frustration. 'How do I know that you won't just wake up one morning and resent my infertility? Rick said he never wanted children, and look what happened with *him*. And with you— you *do* want children!'

'I thought I did,' he said.

Sophie swallowed, her throat suddenly so dry it was like swallowing shards of glass. 'Right,' she said, disbelief sharpening her tone. 'That's not something you can just turn off and on like a light switch.'

'Do you have some experience in that?' he asked, and now looking at him was an impossibility.

She hugged herself, staring unseeingly out at the river, the sun's reflection off its surface making her squint.

'I never had the chance to want children,' she said. 'Remember?'

'The chance to have them and to want them are different things,' he said softly. 'Do you want children?'

She made herself meet his eyes, hurt and confusion warring inside her. Why would he ask her this? The question she'd always pretended didn't exist?

'No. Yes.' A sigh. 'I don't know. I *hate* that I never got the choice. It hurts too much if I think about it.'

That made it a *yes*, she realised.

'So am I enough for you, Sophie?' Dan asked, his eyes still that blue that seemed to see everything—right through into her heart. 'I can't give you children. And if you wanted to adopt there's no guarantee. It would just be you and me.'

'Don't be stupid. It's *my* fault we can't have kids, no—'

'It is *not* your fault,' he said, the ferocity of his quiet tone shocking her into silence. 'And you know what? If that's the price to pay for having you, then that's fine with me. *You* are more important to me than anything else in the world, Sophie.'

This time when he reached for her she didn't shrug him away. His fingers ran down her arm from shoulder to elbow to wrist, linking his fingers with hers.

Slowly his words were seeping in—right through her—despite her efforts to resist.

'So, Sophie—*am* I enough for you? Is my love enough for you?'

Love?

For a moment she was sure her heart stopped beating.

Could he really love her—her alone? It was what he was telling her, but how many ways did he need to say it before she could let herself believe?

He was asking her to love him with the same limitations that life had imposed upon her. To love just him.

But the thing was the depth of emotion she felt for Dan *didn't* have boundaries. In fact it felt limitless.

Was that how he felt about her?

She looked up at him, searching his face for a hint of *something*. Something that would prove what he was saying wasn't real. Something false, something fragile, something unsure.

But there was nothing. The only way she could describe the way he was looking at her was with *love*. Boundaryless, limitless love.

'Yes,' she said, finally allowing the knowledge of Dan's love to thrum in glorious rhythm through her veins. With every beat of her heart she felt that ache, that hollowness inside her, ebb and flow away.

He tugged at her hand, pulling her close. But the tiniest of spaces still separated their bodies as she lost herself in his gaze.

'You know what?' he said. '*Enough* is the wrong word,

Soph. I love you. I want to spend the rest of my life with you. And at the end of all of those days I'll still be wanting more.'

Convinced that if her heart beat any faster it would burst, she reached for him with her free hand, sliding it along the lapel of his jacket and curving it behind his neck. She stood on tiptoes even as she drew him closer. 'I know what you mean,' she said, her lips a breath away from his. 'I love you, too.'

And then she kissed him, with love and with hope as her body shimmered with happiness.

He pulled her tight against him, cradling her with his strength.

When finally they broke apart—just a little—he murmured against her neck, 'So, is for ever something I can interest you in?'

'Just you and me, for ever?'

He caught her chin with his fingers, holding her perfectly still as their gazes locked and held.

'Just you and just me. Just us.'

She smiled, memorising the angles and planes of his handsome face and, most importantly, the way he was looking at her. As if she was the most precious, most beautiful, most amazing thing he'd ever seen.

She'd never felt this way—never thought she could be loved this way.

But it was happening. It was real.

'Yes,' she said. 'For ever suits me just fine.'

Dan smiled at her with joy and with love.

And for the first time ever, no matter how hard she searched, she couldn't locate that perennial emptiness inside her. She didn't feel broken or damaged or faulty.

She was whole.

* * * * *

COMING NEXT MONTH from Harlequin® Romance
AVAILABLE JULY 2, 2012

#4321 THE RANCHER'S HOUSEKEEPER
In Her Shoes...
Rebecca Winters
Rugged rancher Colt Brannigan hires mysterious
Geena Williams as his housekeeper. But is this beautiful
stranger trouble with a capital *T?*

#4322 THE COWBOY COMES HOME
The Larkville Legacy
Patricia Thayer
Single mom Jess Calhoun catches the eye of cowboy
Johnny Jameson. Can this wild wanderer settle down in
sleepy Larkville?

#4323 BATTLE FOR THE SOLDIER'S HEART
Cara Colter
Cynical Rory is drawn to Grace's sweetness. But she
mustn't fall for him—he's all kinds of wrong for her....

#4324 THE LAST WOMAN HE'D EVER DATE
Liz Fielding
Journalist Claire Thackeray wants the inside scoop
on the new owner of Cranbrook Park—her teen crush,
brooding Hal North!

#4325 ONE DAY TO FIND A HUSBAND
The McKenna Brothers
Shirley Jump
Ellie's wish to adopt baby Jiao hits a husband-size
hump! So she proposes a merger-with-a-twist with
business rival Finn McKenna....

#4326 INVITATION TO THE PRINCE'S PALACE
Jennie Adams
Mel's just a normal girl until a cab ride with
Prince Rikardo becomes an invitation to a whole
new life!

REQUEST YOUR FREE BOOKS!
2 FREE NOVELS PLUS 2 FREE GIFTS!

Harlequin

Romance

From the Heart, For the Heart

YES! Please send me 2 FREE Harlequin® Romance novels and my 2 FREE gifts (gifts are worth about $10). After receiving them, if I don't wish to receive any more books, I can return the shipping statement marked "cancel". If I don't cancel, I will receive 6 brand-new novels every month and be billed just $4.09 per book in the U.S. or $4.49 per book in Canada. That's a savings of at least 14% off the cover price! It's quite a bargain! Shipping and handling is just 50¢ per book in the U.S. and 75¢ per book in Canada.* I understand that accepting the 2 free books and gifts places me under no obligation to buy anything. I can always return a shipment and cancel at any time. Even if I never buy another book, the two free books and gifts are mine to keep forever.

116/316 HDN FESE

Name _____ (PLEASE PRINT) _____

Address _____ Apt. #

City _____ State/Prov. _____ Zip/Postal Code

Signature (if under 18, a parent or guardian must sign)

Mail to the **Reader Service:**
IN U.S.A.: P.O. Box 1867, Buffalo, NY 14240-1867
IN CANADA: P.O. Box 609, Fort Erie, Ontario L2A 5X3

Not valid for current subscribers to Harlequin Romance books.

**Are you a subscriber to Harlequin Romance books
and want to receive the larger-print edition?
Call 1-800-873-8635 or visit www.ReaderService.com.**

* Terms and prices subject to change without notice. Prices do not include applicable taxes. Sales tax applicable in N.Y. Canadian residents will be charged applicable taxes. Offer not valid in Quebec. This offer is limited to one order per household. All orders subject to credit approval. Credit or debit balances in a customer's account(s) may be offset by any other outstanding balance owed by or to the customer. Please allow 4 to 6 weeks for delivery. Offer available while quantities last.

Your Privacy—The Reader Service is committed to protecting your privacy. Our Privacy Policy is available online at www.ReaderService.com or upon request from the Reader Service.

We make a portion of our mailing list available to reputable third parties that offer products we believe may interest you. If you prefer that we not exchange your name with third parties, or if you wish to clarify or modify your communication preferences, please visit us at www.ReaderService.com/consumerschoice or write to us at Reader Service Preference Service, P.O. Box 9062, Buffalo, NY 14269. Include your complete name and address.

Harlequin® Romance

A secret letter…two families changed forever

Welcome to Larkville, Texas, where the Calhoun family has been ranching for generations. When Jess Calhoun discovers a secret, unopened letter written to her late father, she learns that there is a whole other branch of her family. Find out what happens when the two sides meet….

A new Larkville Legacy story is available every month beginning July 2012.

Collect all 8 tales!

Patricia Thayer welcomes you to Larkville, Texas, in THE COWBOY COMES HOME—book 1 in the exciting new 8-book miniseries, THE LARKVILLE LEGACY, from Harlequin® Romance.

REACHING THE BANK, Jess climbed down, smiling as she walked her mount to the water. "Wow, I haven't ridden like that in years."

"You're good."

"I'm Clay Calhoun's daughter. I'm supposed to be a good rider."

"You miss him."

She walked with him through the stiff winter grass to the tree. "It's hard to imagine the Double Bar C going on without him. He loved this land." She glanced around the landscape. "Now my brother runs the operation, but he'll be gone awhile." She released a breath. "I have to say we miss his leadership."

He frowned. "Is there anything I can do?"

"Thank you. You're handling Storm—that's a big enough help. It's just that it would be nice to have my brothers and sister here." She looked at him. "Do you have any siblings?"

He shook his head. "None that I know of."

"What about your father?" she asked.

He shook his head. "Never been in my life. I tried for years to track him down, but I never could catch up with him."

He caught the sadness etched on her face. "Johnny, I'm sorry."

He hated pity, especially from her. "Why? You had nothing to do with it. Jake Jameson didn't want to be found, or meet his son." He shrugged. "You can't miss what you've never had. I'm not much of a homebody, either. I guess that's why I like to keep moving."

Jess looked out over the land. "I guess that's where we're different. I've never really moved away from Larkville."

"Why should you want to leave? You have your business here and your home."

She smiled. "I had to fight Dad to live on my own. But I've got a little Calhoun stubbornness, too."

"You got all the beauty."

Johnny came closer, removed her hat and studied her face. "Your eyes are incredible. And your mouth… I could kiss you for hours."

She sucked in a breath and raised her gaze to his. "Johnny… We weren't going to start this."

"Don't look now, darlin', but it's already started."

Find out what happens between Johnny and Jess in
THE COWBOY COMES HOME by Patricia Thayer,
available July 2012!

And find out how Jess's family will be transformed
in the 8-book series:
THE LARKVILLE LEGACY
A secret letter…two families changed forever

Debut author

Kathy Altman

takes you on a moving journey
of forgiveness and second chances.

One year after losing her husband in Afghanistan,
Parker Dean finds Corporal Reid Macfarland at her
door with a heartfelt confession and a promise to save
her family business. Although Reid is the last person
Parker should trust her livelihood to, she finds herself
captivated by his silent courage. Together,
can they learn to forgive and love again?

The Other Soldier

Available July 2012 wherever books are sold.

HSR71790

SPECIAL EDITION

Life, Love and Family

USA TODAY bestselling author

Leanne Banks

begins a heartwarming new miniseries

Royal Babies

When princess Pippa Devereaux learns that the mother of Texas tycoon and longtime business rival Nic Lafitte is terminally ill she secretly goes against her family's wishes and helps Nic fulfill his mother's dying wish. Nic is awed by Pippa's kindness and quickly finds himself falling for her. But can their love break their long-standing family feud?

THE PRINCESS
AND THE OUTLAW

Available July 2012!
Wherever books are sold.

HSE65680